Ravensworth

Ravensworth

Diana R. Tuke

The Pentland Press Limited
Edinburgh • Cambridge • Durham • USA

First published in 2000 by
The Pentland Press Ltd.
1 Hutton Close
South Church
Bishop Auckland
Durham

British Library Cataloguing in Publication Data.
A Catalogue record for this book is available
from the British Library.

ISBN 1 85821 744 X

Typeset by CBS, Martlesham Heath, Ipswich, Suffolk
Printed and bound by Bookcraft Ltd, Bath

In memory of my treasured parents.

AUTHOR'S NOTE

Although I have used real places and place names throughout this book, and historical names and events appear, it is fiction, and Ravensworth – the village, estate and family, together with all the other characters – will only be found within its pages.

D.R.T.

FOREWORD

This charming story traces the history of the Ravensworth family over several generations. Set in the Cotswolds with fascinating insights into the countryside the reader is swept along by the fortunes and indeed misfortunes of various members of the family.

The large family estate at Ravensworth Towers gives a vivid background throughout and the reader is able to join in with the hopes and fears of parents and children throughout different periods of their lives.

The author's thorough understanding of the countryside and the many rural issues which affected the lives of those at the time makes the reader very aware of the historical factors which influenced the different generations.

Idyllic childhood days during the Victorian era leading swiftly through hunting parties, country fetes, point to points and on to the worries of war and the affect this had on the fortunes of the family are told in a caring moving way. It seems that Diana Tuke is reliving many of her own memories of certain periods of her life giving the book a particularly warm and graphic flashback into the past.

The fortunes of the family and the estate and the essentially Tudor house demonstrate all too clearly how difficult it was for so many families to move into a more modern world and be able to maintain such places which enrich the British countryside. This story shows how one family managed to change course when times became less good, diversify and with ingenuity set up a country hotel.

The book is a good read and very enjoyable with well told flashbacks and nostalgic anecdotes throughout which leaves one sorry when it comes to an end yet glad you have been able to share the experiences within the Ravensworth world.

Jane Holderness-Roddam LVO

THE RAVENSWORTH FAMILY TREE

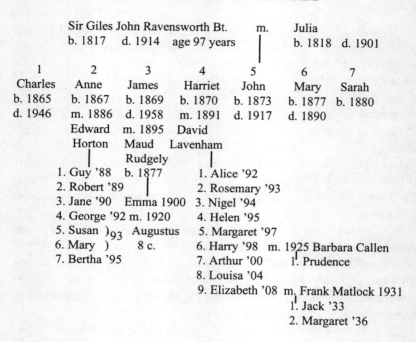

Sir Giles John Ravensworth Bt.   m.   Julia
b. 1817   d. 1914   age 97 years   b. 1818 d. 1901

1	2	3	4	5	6	7
Charles	Anne	James	Harriet	John	Mary	Sarah
b. 1865	b. 1867	b. 1869	b. 1870	b. 1873	b. 1877	b. 1880
d. 1946	m. 1886	d. 1958	m. 1891	d. 1917	d. 1890	

Edward   m. 1895 David
Horton   Maud   Lavenham
       Rudgely

1. Guy '88   b. 1877   1. Alice '92
2. Robert '89   2. Rosemary '93
3. Jane '90   Emma 1900   3. Nigel '94
4. George '92 m. 1920   4. Helen '95
5. Susan ⎫93 Augustus   5. Margaret '97
6. Mary ⎭   8 c.   6. Harry '98 m. 1925 Barbara Callen
7. Bertha '95   7. Arthur '00   1. Prudence
                            8. Louisa '04
                            9. Elizabeth '08 m. Frank Matlock 1931
                                        1. Jack '33
                                        2. Margaret '36

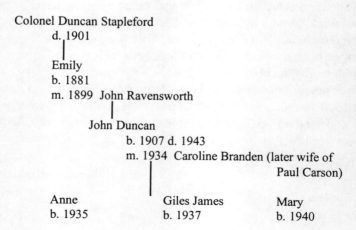

Colonel Duncan Stapleford
d. 1901

Emily
b. 1881
m. 1899 John Ravensworth

John Duncan
b. 1907 d. 1943
m. 1934 Caroline Branden (later wife of
                      Paul Carson)

Anne   Giles James   Mary
b. 1935   b. 1937   b. 1940

Chapter I

The morning sun filtered through the creeper that grew in profusion round the leaded diamond panes of the hall window, and fell in shafts on the old stone hearth. Pickles stretched, yawned, and curled up again in its warmth. He was a lazy cat and loved to sleep the morning through, in the peace and comfort of the hall. Later, his morning nap might be disturbed, and he would be forced to move kitchenwards, but until that moment, he preferred to remain, lulled into security by the rhythmic hum of the carpet cleaner on the floor above and the steady crackle of the blazing logs on the old stone hearth. He was sleeping the sleep of the peaceful. Admittedly, he had an Aga in the kitchen, but what good to him was that, when busy feet flew in all directions at ninety miles an hour. In fact, it was positively dangerous!

Emily Ravensworth, an old lady now, was engaged upstairs, supervising the preparations for the coming week-end. In the days of long ago, when her father-in-law and brother-in-law had held office and had reigned in turn at the Towers, it had been the venue for the opening meet. Those days were long since past, but to-morrow would see the long delayed revival of the age old custom, and the culmination of many months of hard work on the part of the young Ravensworths and their grandmother. From now until March, every week-end it would be full with hunting folk; for the Towers had proved an undreamt-of success. In a desire to save the Towers, they had hit on the idea of running it as a country hotel. Throughout their first summer, since opening at Easter, they had been comfortably full, their guests returning happily for more and more visits in the peace of the Cotswolds, glad of the chance to escape from the hustle and bustle of

1

the city, even for a week-end. The joy of being able to relax in the quiet comfort of a large country house had drawn many to the Towers. The situation was ideal. The tree-studded park ranged far away into the distance over undulating valleys. Through one of these, the long drive wound its way up to the house. Taking its leisurely time, it passed the lake and bridged the river, before going up the last hill to the tower which straddled the gate-house and gave way to the gravel beyond and the fine old Cotswold manor. Its heavily studded, oak front door added to the charm of the gabled façade, so typical of houses in the Cotswolds. It was behind this door that Pickles was taking his morning nap.

Satisfied everything was in order, Emily moved briskly along the landing towards the linen-room, pausing as she did so at the long low window which looked out over the drive. In the distance, away down the valley, a movement caught her eye and held her attention. On the bend, a car had halted in the drive, and leaning down from his saddle, her grandson Giles, a tall striking lad of twenty-two, was talking to the driver; no doubt they were asking the way, as they often did. People curious to see what lay beyond the gates would drive up to the house, spin round on the gravel and vanish again, to the intense fury of old Moss, the gardener. He took it as a personal insult to his freshly raked gravel, and would brandish his rake after the disappearing offender. As Emily watched, Giles looked up towards the house and waved his stick in the general direction of the buildings; then pulling back from the car, he waved gaily and swinging away, cantered off in the direction of the home farm.

The estate, which included the home farm, was the concern of young Giles Ravensworth. He loved the work and found it intensely interesting. Coming out of the army after his National Service, he had thrown himself wholeheartedly into the great project that lay ahead. The venture was undoubtedly a challenge, a challenge which he and his two sisters, Anne and Mary, had, in a moment of madness, decided to accept. Feeling at a loose end one week-end he had driven over to see a pal at an air-station on the edge of the Cotswolds; and from there they had driven up to see his old family home, twenty miles further north. For a long time he had been wanting to see it again, and now was his chance. How nearly he had regretted his impulsive move; then the old place seemed to cry out to him to rescue it from its dilapidation. On his return to his own camp, he wrote an urgent letter to his elder sister Anne, requesting her to join him at the Towers the following Sunday. Faithful to the summons, she had arrived. It was during that afternoon that the Ravensworth Towers Country Hotel was born.

It was one thing to vow to save their home, but quite another thing to carry it out. Their great-uncle Charles' death had set a poser. Who was the heir? For nearly ten years the legal search had been going on. Their father had only been the son of the youngest son; somewhere, but no one knew where, was the family of great-uncle James. Not long after his marriage to their great-aunt Maud, he had left the country and subsequently been lost touch with. It had taken their grandmother to beard the trustees in their den. Even they could not hold out against the downright old lady for long. Nothing, these days, easily deterred her from any project she had undertaken. In due course the trustees had given the go ahead for the restoration of the Towers. The work had taken a long time, just over two years in fact, but while it was in progress, under the eagle eye of Grandmother, the younger generation had not been idle. Giles had spent his time at Cirencester, learning the estate side from A to Z, while Anne, having already completed a secretarial course, went on to do one in hotel management, leaving Mary to finish her time at school before going to the Cordon Bleu. After all, as Mary had said when told of the plans for the Towers, it was essential to have good cooking if they were to succeed.

What a long time ago all that seemed now, as Giles made the rounds of all the hunt jumps on the estate! During the summer all the flagged jumps in the stonewalls and fences had been wired up; now the wire had been removed. Giles had issued his orders several days before, but he was leaving nothing to chance: his whole reputation depended on the success of their first opening meet.

'Come on, Rustler, we'll cut through here, old boy, and go round by Furze Copse.' Gathering his big chestnut hunter together as he spoke, Giles jumped the stone wall out of the park into the lane that bordered it and ran round the back of the copse to the stable yard and garages near the kitchen windows, about a mile further on. Landing in the lane, Giles pulled up and waited for his young labrador, Bracken, to reach them, before continuing on his way.

Anne, working in the kitchen, looked up as her brother rode into the yard, and waved. Her rather solemn face was at long last beginning to show some true glimmer of happiness. Unlike their mother, who had been beautiful, Anne as a child had been plain and gawky, with two long pig-tails hanging limply down her back. No one, even in charity, could have said they suited her. It had taken their grandmother to remove the monstrosities, shortly after her first meeting with Anne. When she had finished, Anne had been transformed into another person. Still solemn, she now had a quiet distinction of her own. As she grew up, her tall willowy form, with its sharp face, lost its hard, plain look and took on a shy charm of its own. Her mousey hair curled round her high forehead, framing her brown eyes; falling back behind her ears into the nape of her neck, it gave her a pixie look.

'Hello Giles, coming in? Coffee's ready.'

'In a jiffy; I'll just take Rustler round to Paddy.'

'See anything?' asked Anne a few minutes later as her brother kicked off his boots in the doorway. Looking up from the tray she was preparing, she lifted her eyebrow.

'Not really – some old lady asked the way to Sir Charles' house!'

'What did you tell her?' Anne fixed her brother's eye; she knew his sense of humour.

'Oh, just told her she had passed the real turning; but if she cared to go up to the Towers, she could leave the car there and walk along the path that skirts the shrubbery.' Giles grinned and helped himself to a doughnut, still warm and irresistible from Mary's latest batch; and popped it into his mouth, precluding any further conversation.

'Giles! You must stop saying that,' exclaimed Anne in mock horror.

'What will people think of us, if we send everyone to the church who asks for Uncle Charles?'

Wrinkling up his face like a monkey, Giles looked at his sister.

'What of it? It's true! Anyway, where's our sister gone? What's she planning for lunch?'

'A choice of cold salmon or game-pie, with steamed treacle pudding

4

or apple fritters to follow. We don't expect many in to lunch, so she is saving those pheasants till Sunday. At the moment she's out in the hall taking an order, I fancy, from your old lady!'

Pickles purred in his sleep, and cocked an ear. His hearing was acute. Was it a mouse? Or was it a dream? Out on the gravel, footsteps approached. They paused, shuffled, and then proceeded to the door. In the distance, a car rattled over the grid and gathered speed, before the noise died away.

Up in the linen-room, the noise only penetrated the thick walls faintly. No guests were expected before the afternoon at the earliest, so dismissing the car as a tradesman, Emily carried on with her work of sorting the laundry. She was a meticulous worker and was extremely engrossed.

The solid oak door was stiff with age. The old lady found it all she could do to open it. How well she remembered the old bellpull on the wall; but she was reluctant to ring it. All the way from the station, Maud had tried to recall the house she had left so long ago. She was spry and young then; now she was old and crippled with arthritis. Never-the-less she was still alert, and possessed an ardent desire to gaze uninterrupted at the old house. With this aim in view, she had dismissed her taxi at the tower, and walked across the gravel at leisure. At first the young man on the horse had puzzled her with his odd remark. She knew of old that that particular path led across the park to the church by the village.

'Why ma'am, didn't you know? This place is no longer a private house. It's a country hotel,' remarked the driver as they left Giles. 'I bring many people up here. It's very good.'

Maud at first was too stunned to think, then by degrees the big notice by the main gate dawned on her. It had been a discreet sign, showing quiet, good taste, with the words carved out on an oak board, 'RAVENSWORTH TOWERS COUNTRY HOTEL'. Their meaning had passed unnoticed by the old lady, whose every nerve strained towards the house itself. For a moment she nearly turned back, but something drove her on.

'Thank you. Drive on, please, and put me down by the tower.'

What the driver thought, she knew not, and cared less. She was going to see the house now she had come so far.

With a creak, the big door swung inwards and Maud found herself standing once more upon the threshold. Tears welled up in her eyes and ran slowly down her wrinkled face. Quickly she blinked them away. What a sentimental old fool she was! Even so, it was like walking back into the past. Outwardly, the place had not changed. Admittedly, the furnishings were new, but then after all these years they would be. Her eyes wandered lovingly round the panelled walls, and alighted first on the grandfather clock, still in its old place beside the staircase, then on the cat curled in front of a roaring log fire. The sun played its patterns on his tabby back. Pickles took not the slightest notice; he was immune to these interruptions to his morning nap. Crossing the hall to the welcoming fire, Maud paused by the cat and bent down to tickle him behind the ear.

'Well, puss, what do I do? Ring?'

Pickles twitched his ear and yawned.

'Thank you.' The old lady smiled and leant across to the red tassel she remembered so well, and gave it a vigorous tug. Satisfied, she retired to an arm-chair beside the blaze and awaited the outcome, lost in thoughts of the past.

Through the long passages, the bell tolled loudly. Electric bells had been fitted to all the bedrooms, but Emily had retained the others in the downstairs rooms; they were more in keeping with their old world surroundings.

'I'll go,' called Mary, whipping off her apron and fleeing down the passage, pushing her hair back as she went. Giving it a last pat into place, she slowed down and walked quietly through the archway into the hall. Mary's likeness to her brother and sister ended with her colouring; taller than Anne, she had a round cheerful face, and wide set honest eyes that regarded a stranger unblinkingly. It was always fun to speculate on who could have rung. How seldom any of them were right! Mary herself had soon grown used to the scrutiny that followed the encounter with so many visitors to their hotel; but never before had she had to undergo one quite like the one that met her now, out of the green, sunken eyes of the old lady by the fire. It was quite uncanny. On her entry, the old lady had appeared asleep. But this was only an illusion. In fact Maud was very much awake, merely looking back into the past; now she was very much in the present, taking in every detail. Neither broke the silence for a brief second, till Mary pulled herself together sharply.

Their voices floated up the well of the stairs and drifted along to the linen-room where Emily was still busy. She paused; surely she knew that second voice. As if by magic, the years rolled back to the days of her girlhood. Quickly she put down the pillow-cases she was counting, and softly opened the door. The voices were clearer now. Mary was evidently undergoing a cross-examination. With measured tread, Emily made her way to the head of the stairs and peered down the deep well, which afforded her an excellent view of the hall, from wall to wall, She blinked – looked again – and as she stared down, her eyes grew larger and larger; surely the years were playing tricks with her sight and hearing, it was impossible; it could not be true. But it was. There below sat her sister-in-law as large as life. Even after all these years, Emily could not forget that tilt of the head and odd lilt to her voice when she was asking a question. It was so birdlike. With a chuckle, instead of going straight down the main staircase, Emily retraced her steps to the secondary stairs that led straight to the kitchens.

'All right, Anne, I'll take that, my dear.' There was a definite twinkle in Emily's eyes as she picked up the tray Anne had been preparing so carefully, 'Where's Mary?'

'She came in here, gave the order, and then mumbled something about having to find Giles at once. Can't think what's bitten her. Looked as if she had just seen a ghost or something.'

It was Anne's turn to stare at her grandmother now. The coffee time waiting was her job, or else Mary's, but never their grandmother's; this had been part of the bargain.

What was going on out there in the hall? Anne was consumed with burning curiosity, as she watched her grandmother bear the tray off with evident satisfaction and an extremely purposeful manner. Mary had merely said,

'Coffee for Mrs James in the hall.' Anne shrugged her shoulders and turned back to her work. Shortly, unless someone let her into the secret, she would be forced to find some excuse to go through the hall and see this mysterious Mrs James for herself. Granny, no doubt, had been listening from the landing!

Chapter II

Old Mrs Moss, the wife of the gardener, had been a godsend to the young Ravensworths when they had taken their big plunge. A real treasure, she came every morning to exert her still considerable energies in whatever direction they might be required. This morning, she was bustling round the outer kitchen preparing the vegetables for lunch, at the same time keeping a weather ear open for any tit-bits. She was to be disappointed, for Anne knew no more than she did. Leaving them together, Emily proceeded on her stately way towards the hall.

A lofty, heavily beamed room, it had always been furnished to sit in, having plenty of easy chairs and small tables, besides the larger, less comfortable pieces of furniture that lined the walls. During the lengthy restoration work, Emily had been loath to alter anything that was not absolutely necessary. She had been delighted with the outcome, for the Towers needed every inch of room it had, and the hall had proved one of the most popular rooms in the whole hotel. The casual visitors liked to sit there after a meal and drink their coffee, for in summer it was cool, and in winter, the large log fire bade welcome to those coming in from the wind-swept Cotswolds.

Rounding the archway, Emily stopped, surveying the scene before her eyes. How many years had lapsed since her first meeting with Maud? Standing there just out of sight, Emily gave a slow smile. How little she had ever expected to see her sister-in-law again after her departure with James for the New World, fifty-two years ago! Much water had flowed under the bridge since then and the years had left their mark on the once beautiful features of Maud Rudgely,

9

Looking at her now, reclining in her chair by the fire, her face showed the wrinkles and ageing brought on by disappointment and sadness. The wrench must have been hard for her to leave her homeland and her family and set off on an expedition into the unknown. Still young, they had gone with bitter resentment as their companion and guide. Never for one moment did either of them expect Sir Giles to keep his word, and they were horrified when he did. It had bitten into the very depths of their hearts; though Maud forgave, James never did. From the day of their departure, he never wrote to his father again. It had brought pain and sorrow to many. Emily hated, even now, to think of that departure, and preferred to remember the happy family occasion of their wedding two years before.

Straightening her shoulders, Emily took a step forward into the room.

'Good morning, Maud.'

Maud jumped, and looked round in bewilderment. She, too, knew that voice out of the past. Looking up she met a pair of twinkling eyes. Carefully, Emily set the tray down on a small table beside Maud's chair.

'Why – Emily – what's the meaning of that!' She pointed at the tray.

'Why are you here!?'

'Waiting!'

'For what?'

'On you.'

'How do you mean? You can't mean you are actually a waitress?' Maud's eyes gazed sharply at the younger woman in pure disbelief.

'Well, yes and no. You see, this is our hotel; so I suppose you could call me a manageress. A bit different from the old days, aye? But then times have changed. No one in England can afford to run a house of this size without doing something to help it on its way. It's a very long story, but please don't let your coffee get cold.'

'Won't you join me, Emily? Do sit down, I want to talk to you.'

'All right, I'll just ring for Anne and ask her to bring some more cups. She's my eldest grandchild.' Moving across to the bell pull, Emily gave it two sharp tugs that sent a resounding peal through to

Anne, a sign to Anne to come herself.

Hearing the summons, Anne quickly whipped off her apron and tidied herself, her mind full of curiosity.

'Please tell Mary I've gone to the hall, if she should come in.'

'All right, Miss,' called Mrs Moss from the outer kitchen. She was a rotund little body, who in the days of her great-grandfather had been a tweeny, while Moss had been the gardener's boy, born and bred on the estate. It had been with tremendous pleasure that they had returned to work once more for the family they had served for so long. Even in their old age, with so many changes to the estate, they found peace in the work they knew, and a delight in their home in the gate-tower lodge.

'Oh, there you are.' Emily looked up fondly at her grand-daughter and smiled as the girl entered the hall. 'Come here, my dear.'

Anne crossed to her grandmother's side, picking her way carefully over Pickles still asleep on the hearth-rug, purring rhythmically in the heat of the blazing logs. He was sleeping the sleep of a well-fed, contented puss.

'Anne, I want you to meet your great-aunt, Maud.' Emily watched to see what reaction these words would have on the girl.

Anne looked down into the green sunken eyes and then as if by instinct, she bent swiftly, and kissed the wrinkled old cheek. The old lady's arms, stiff and arthritic, came up and clung to the young girl with surprising strength. Eventually the old lady released her, and Anne sank down beside her great-aunt, at her feet, looking up at first one face and then the other, waiting for an explanation.

'Hallo, Mrs Moss, where's my sister please?' Giles poked his head through the window.

'Through in the hall, Master Giles; Mrs Ravensworth sent for her about five minutes gone!' replied Mrs Moss, attacking the eyes in a potato she was peeling with vigour. Her face was a study. She sensed something unusual was afoot and she was dying to know what it was. Her words were charged with meaning. Giles smiled to himself; how well he knew her in this mood.

'Thanks.' Coming in, Giles kicked off his boots and paddled across the floor in search of his shoes. Bracken had yet to learn to leave

11

such nice commodities alone. She was only a young dog, and had a predilection for anything left lying around, especially if it was soft.

'No, Giles!' wailed Mary from the doorway behind him. 'Not in here.'

'What? Bracken? Oh, she's all right. Come here, girl. Give. Good dog, dead! Look, she's learning!' Giles looked up grinning at his younger sister's face as he bent and patted his dog. 'She's not as bad as she looks; she only went for a swim in the lake on the way up. She'll dry.'

Anne chose this moment to come back into the kitchen in search of the other members of her family, her eyes ablaze with excitement.

'Here, you two! Guess who the old lady is out in the hall?'

Quickly, Anne unfolded her story, while she gathered up some more cups and saucers, as well as biscuits and coffee. Leading the way, they all returned to the hall, Bracken, unnoticed, bringing up the rear. She was an affable dog, and loved nothing better than to get loose among the visitors in the main part of the house, where they were inclined to spoil her. She was very apt to slip through, if she knew anyone was in the hall, coming round the hall entrance, waggling her whole body and rolling her big, speaking eyes. To-day, she walked with measured tread till they reached the hall. Bounding forward, she rushed wildly across the intervening space that separated her from Aunt Maud, on whose lap Pickles now reclined in comfort. Startled, he sat up, arched his back, and spat, issuing a sharp hissing sound from his wide-open mouth and dealing a deft blow to Bracken's nose with his paw, all claws fully extended, for good measure. With a yelp, Bracken shot backwards, cannoning into Emily's chair.

'Giles! Please remove your dog!' Granny was not pleased!

'Oh, Gran, Bracken is all right. It was Pickles. Come here, sit.'

Waggling her quarters, Bracken slunk over to her owner and sat down, sweeping the floor with her tail with great vigour, her eyes pleading forgiveness.

'No, Emily. Please don't banish the dog, I like her. So this is Giles, is it?' Her green eyes twinkled. 'How like your grandfather you are. I wondered who you could be, when we met earlier.' Giles could swear that those eyes were dancing with appreciation, and grinned sheepishly, as the old lady turned her attention to the youngest member of the family.

'And Mary. Well, well!' Without waiting for further conversation, Mary too sank down beside her great-aunt's chair, having first kissed the old lady kindly. It was strange to come face to face with her after all these years, having heard so much about her and Uncle James.

'You're staying, aren't you, Aunt?' Giles looked across from his perch on the window-sill, which was furnished with cushions to form a comfortable window-seat, overlooking the gravel. 'We've room, haven't we, Anne?'

'Oh, yes, that's settled. Aunt Maud is having my room, and I'm going in with Mary.' Anne spoke with conviction in her voice as she turned to her sister. 'That's all right, isn't it, Mary?'

'Of course. Good Lord, yes, I don't mind. Are we full though?'

'Yes, that Mrs Otley, who was here in the summer, rang this morning and asked if we could let her have another room for her son. He's got some leave or something, and wants to come down, too. They're bringing another horse. I rang Jill, and she can take it. Thank heavens; we don't want it here. The Mantons are only bringing two now, which makes room for the other one of the Otleys. I must say, Jill's stables are going to be most useful this season.'

'What room have you given him?' inquired Mary, pouring out more coffee.

'The little single room up in the west wing. It's small, but it is rather nice, and will have to do. We just haven't another.' As she spoke, Anne felt a feeling of quiet satisfaction creep over her; they were full, not another soul could they squeeze in!

Aunt Maud, instead of being bored by all these business details, was, on the contrary, extremely interested, and plied Emily and the children (if we may call them that still, though they were, in fact, now all grown up, even if they remained children to Emily and Maud) with more and more questions, each one leading to another, till they were dizzy.

It would have gone on indefinitely, had not Giles glanced at his watch and exclaimed, 'Gosh! Is that the time? Please excuse me, Aunt Maud, I've got to run down to the station. By the way, where's your luggage? If it's down there, I'll bring it up for you.'

There was a scrunch on the gravel as a car sped round the house, followed by a rattle, and Giles was gone in a cloud of dust.

The two old ladies then found themselves once more alone. Giles' departure had brought the girls back to the present and they had followed their brother from the hall, leaving their grandmother to Maud's mercy. Together the sisters went upstairs to prepare Anne's room for their aunt. It was a pretty little room up in what had been the nursery wing. Emily had taken the wing over for their own use. Unlike the rest of the house, it was only on two floors, with the kitchens underneath and the eaves coming down like an egg-cosy in their own rooms. The wing had lent itself to its present use very well indeed, for it had provided the Ravensworths with four bedrooms, a bathroom, and a delightful sitting room of their own, in what had once been the day nursery. The room was light and roomy and looked out over the park. It was well remembered by Emily from her childhood days at the Towers. With loving care she had transformed the room into what it was to-day, a haven of rest away from the rest of the house, where she could creep and escape from the exigencies of life in a busy hotel, when the pace became too much for her to cope with in her old age; not that this was often, thank heavens, but all the same she liked to feel she had a place of refuge when she needed it. It was like the old days, when she had first visited the Towers as a very small girl in the early 1890s. How she had loved to come up to the big room and join her small friends. It had opened out a new and exciting life to the small girl from India, who had never known the joy of companionship before. It was a new and happy world in which she was content and safe.

For Maud, the room could never hold quite the same significance, for her visits to the Towers had been rare. All the same she had been fond of the old house and all the memories she had taken with her had been happy ones, save for the last parting one, which had been sad. In the days directly before her wedding, she had been a frequent visitor, and had never failed to visit the nursery where at least some of Sir Giles' grandchildren were to be found. The old man was fond of children, and would gather his own round him, till the place was full.

A luxury that Emily had installed during the restoration work was a small, automatic, passenger lift. It was simple and such a blessing, for besides saving the legs of the elderly guests, it also saved Emily's when she became tired. Many had returned because of it. Cleverly sited, Emily had had it installed in a small alcove which might have been made for it, so neatly did it tuck away round the corner, alongside the telephones and out of sight, just off the main hall. Its original use had long since faded into obscurity, even from Emily's remarkable memory; but Maud soon found the use to which the alcove had been put, and commented with pleasure on her foresight.

'Why, this is cute!'

With the aid of the lift, Maud was soon shuffling along the many passages and peeping into long forgotten places. Her explorations took in every inch of the old place.

'Well, Emily, my dear, don't bother about me. Are the rooms empty? If so, may I please go where I like? I would just like to take my time and wander around quietly and take the place in in my own time.'

'Why, certainly, you may. Go just where you like, We are empty; the first guests are not due until after lunch. If you will excuse me, I must leave you, for I have rather a lot to do between then and now. But do tell me if there is anything I can do for you, or you want to know.'

Leaving her sister-in-law, Emily walked briskly along the narrow hall that led to the big drawing-room, a delightful room that looked out over the south lawns, to the ha-ha and park beyond. Down in the valley, the lake was shimmering in the sunlight. Along its edge grew tall, slender silver birches, waving gracefully in the breeze, throwing their shadows on the backs of the small herd of tame deer that roamed at will in the park.

The deer, like the ravens that lived in the gate-house tower, were part of the Ravensworth estate, having lived there from time immemorial.

Ravensworth Towers dated back to Tudor times, when the Ravensworth of the day demolished the existing mansion and re-built it on the same site, incorporating a few of the finer features of the old building into the Tudor design. The roiling park that surrounded the gracious house became the home of a famous herd of deer, whose renown spread throughout the land. Unfortunately, their numbers were drastically reduced soon afterwards, for Her Majesty had a passion for hunting, and expressed a royal wish to hunt in these wide acres. Many years were to pass before the herd regained its former strength, but even now, in these altered times, a small herd remained. They were a pretty sight, and on the whole, caused very little damage. The Ravensworths would never dream of parting with them, for they made the place.

At tea-time, the house, quiet all day except for a few lunchtime visitors, woke up and became alive. Footsteps echoed through the rooms and passages, doors slammed, voices rang out in happy chatter. Thirty-six guests that night sat down to dinner, but only thirty could be accommodated in the Towers itself. They always had a proportion of casual visitors and to-night was no exception. Sue and Fanny, who came up from the village to wait, were busy from seven-thirty till after ten. As late as nine-thirty the last guests put in an appearance, full of apologies for their car having broken down some miles back. With their guests gravitating towards the bar after dinner, the noise increased; old friends greeted one another, and met new ones, all with a common interest. Once a small study, the bar was extremely cosy with a blazing log fire and a tiny bar tucked in across one corner. There was a friendly atmosphere that prevailed throughout the hotel and, though Giles usually ran the bar himself, enjoying the congenial company, the girls also gave a hand and were to be found there when they were very busy.

Maud, tired after her long day, bade the family good-night soon after dinner and retired to her room, promising to see them all at breakfast.

Chapter III

Brr – Brr! the alarm clock danced on the table beside Mary's bed. Mary rolled over and stretched out an arm to clout it. The noise stopped abruptly. Then rolling back, Mary ducked under the bed-clothes again for a brief second, calling out to her sister as she did so.

'Anne, Anne, wake up, it's five!'

Anne yawned, stretched and sat up gingerly, kicking off the bed-clothes at the same time, before rolling out of the low camp-bed. This was the only safe way in which to achieve this difficult task. Once out, she stood up.

'Well, come on, you've got to get up too, lazybones.' Mary opened one eye and closed it again. The morning was cold. November had come in with a suspicion of a frost. 'Who's waking Giles?'

'I will, on my way to the bathroom.' Mary leapt out of bed and grabbed her dressing gown from the foot of her bed, vanishing out of the door as she tugged it on. Anne smiled to herself; in six hours time, hounds would move off! The sky was still black as night as she poked her nose through the curtains to see what the day had to offer. Sharply she drew it in again. Outside was not welcoming. Down in the stable yard, the sound of a horse stamping echoed up to the girls, and was followed by another rattling a bucket. They too, were waking. Soon Paddy O'Doo would be out there grooming and feeding his favourites, before plaiting them ready for the opening meet later in the morning. Besides the Ravensworths' own horses, which were stabled in the main block on their own, another block had been set aside for the use of the guests, who could stable their hunters there if they wished, provided they either sent their own grooms or looked

17

after them themselves; otherwise, their horses were to go down to the village to Jill's stables. This arrangement looked like working very well.

Mary could hardly believe that at long last she could really hunt regularly. Up till now, owing to school, she had only had the holidays in which to go out. These had been short and often the weather had put a stop to hunting, just when she was at home. Throughout her young life, she had been a member of the local Pony Club, and still belonged to the Ravensworth branch, having another year to run. Giles and Anne had also spent their young days in the Pony Club and had gained most of their knowledge from it; now they both helped to run their local branch. At last, with hunters of their own, they were able to look forward to a life they loved. With the hotel to fill their lives, their horses provided recreation and pleasure. It would be hard to picture Ravensworth without horses, for the Ravensworths and horses were synonymous.

Soon the kitchen was a hive of activity. Row upon row of small trays lined the long dresser, each with its own small brown tea-pot, milk jug, sugar basin and plate of biscuits besides its cup and saucer. The secret of their success lay in the fact that they went to infinite trouble over the small things. Nothing was too much bother, provided it looked nice in the end. The morning trays were both dainty and appetizing, the brown ware toning with its surroundings and décor.

'I'll do the milk, if you do the biscuits,' called Anne, going to the fridge. Emily had had the good sense to install the best available equipment in the kitchen, when, with the rest of the place, it underwent its modernization. It was hard to realize just what it had been like before Emily had been let loose to use her ingenuity; she had made the place charming, with blue the predominating colour in the curtains and floors, leaving the rest a crisp white. The effect was one of cool cleanliness, in a room which otherwise would soon have become oppressive and stuffy.

With the melodious chimes of the grandfather clock dying away, Anne and Mary, laden with trays, started off on their morning rounds, punctually at seven. Experience had taught them how to negotiate the stairs and passages through which they had to go, in order to

18

reach all the guests who required morning tea.

The mornings were the hardest time of the day, when the girls tackled everything alone. Sue and Fanny only came in time to lay the tables for lunch; while Mrs Moss did not put in her first appearance till breakfast had finished. They were stalwart workers, but even so it was necessary to employ three more women from the village to help clean. Indoors, save for the help of old Morpeth, Uncle Charles' butler, this was all. Like Mr and Mrs Moss, Morpeth was an institution and would have a job at the Towers as long as he required it. He would toddle in from his cottage at the back of the house and spend his time cleaning silver and doing other jobs without being asked. Beyond this, the Ravensworths had no other help, though there was an outside staff under Giles' supervision.

Breakfasting early, the three young Ravensworths had always finished by the time the guests came down for theirs. In this and this alone, were they able to rule their grandmother. On no account would they sanction her early rising or breakfasting in the kitchen. After all, she was seventy-eight, and no longer as young as she had been. Nevertheless, the old lady was the first in the dining-room. No one had yet beaten her to it. She was grateful to her grandchildren for their evident concern for her well being. They were good to her, and did their best to let her live very much the life she had always led in the days gone by at the Towers. Maud, too, was a good riser, and soon joined Emily in the dining-room, looking refreshed from her night's sleep.

'Good morning, Maud. Sleep well?'

'Yes, thank you, Emily. And you?'

'Thank you; I always sleep well.'

These punctilious greetings having been exchanged, both old ladies relapsed into silence. The silence was only broken when Mary bore in coffee on a tray.

'Good morning, Aunt Maud, Grandmother.' Mary slid the tray onto the table with a practised hand. Smiling she turned away, only to feel a bony hand come out and grip her arm.

'Not hunting? Why not, my dear?'

'Oh yes, I am; we all are!' Mary's eyes danced. 'But who's ever heard of a waitress in breeches and a stock serving breakfast, even to hunting folk!' Mary's chuckle was remarkably like her grandmother's.

Aunt Maud looked first startled; then shocked; and lastly to Mary's relief, for she was beginning to feel uncomfortable, her great-aunt laughed, and wagged a finger at her niece.

'Naughty girl!'

By half-past ten, the dining-room was once more empty. In less than half-an-hour the gravel would be crowded with horses and people, both mounted and on foot. November the seventh had dawned fine and crisp, the type of morning that sends a tingle through one, of sheer pleasure and expectancy, and sends the horses dancing and fidgeting all over the place. Even the staid old hunters play with their bits and snort.

Everywhere, men and women, young and old, were hurrying in all directions, calling to one another. One had lost her whip and another had mislaid her spurs. At one moment, the high shrill voice of a young girl could be heard calling to a friend for her cap.

Slowly the hall began to fill with riders, all neat and tidy, some in pink, some in black coats, their top boots and spurs shining, but soon to be splattered with mud. On the big round table in the middle of the hall lay a pile of packets, each containing sandwiches. No wonder Anne and Mary were hot and tired as they flew upstairs to their own quarters.

'Bless Granny. Look, she's put out all our things,' cried Anne, pushing open Mary's door.

Frantically, both girls stripped off their things and clambered into their shirts and breeches. Holding their breath, they tied their stocks, for there was no time to waste on making mistakes this morning. Satisfied, the boots followed and lastly their black coats and caps.

'Ready; right, come on.' Mary was already out of the room.

About half the field had arrived by the time the girls had dressed. Rushing down to the hall, they met Giles carrying a tray laden with drinks. Looking at the two girls, he smiled, a happy cheerful smile. In their turn, the girls gazed at their brother; this was the first time they had seen him in a pink coat, and undoubtedly it suited his tall, lean figure. All round them, the air was charged with excitement. Soon both girls forgot they had ever been tired, and were dashing here, there and everywhere, giving Giles and old Morpeth a hand with the drinks. Horses, now streaming in through the gate-house tower, packed the gravel outside the front door. The grid, for the occasion, had been closed. This was an ingenious affair; in the gate-house was a lever that could either close or open the grid at will. All that had to be done was for the lever to be pulled to the right or left, and then locked in the required position. When closed, the grid became a solid metal ramp, on which was spread peat-moss to deaden the clatter of several hundred hooves.

A prominent person at the meet that morning was Great-aunt Maud. Walking with the aid of a stick, the old lady progressed from one person to another, talking happily of bygone days. It was surprising how many faces in that vast gathering she remembered, especially among the village folk and tenants of the estate. Somehow, in the extraordinary way news spreads in the country, the word had gone round that Mrs James was home again. On all sides a warm welcome was extended to the old lady, who beamed and smiled in pleasure.

For Emily too, the day was a very special one. As spry as ever, dressed in her favourite tweeds and a 'country' felt that denoted her generation, she accepted the congratulations extended to her with graceful dignity, passing among her friends, chatting happily, unaware of anything unusual. From across the gravel, old Jim picked his way carefully among the horses, towards the front door. Advanced in years, Jim still lived near his beloved hounds and rarely missed seeing them hunt the home coverts. His whole life had been spent among the Ravensworth hounds, working his way up, after leaving school, from kennel boy to the post of first whip and kennel huntsman under Sir Charles. But in the days when he first remembered Emily, Sir Giles had been master and Emily a small girl on a pony, while he had just been promoted to second whip. Reaching his goal, he cleared his throat, a signal to the field to stop their chatter. With a small bow, he turned to Emily.

'Ma'am; on behalf of the Hunt and the Ravensworth estate, it would give us much pleasure if you would accept this small memento of the

sixtieth anniversary of the opening meet following your marriage.
Our only regret is that your husband can no longer be with us.'

Emily stared blankly, too touched even to speak. Little had she
realized in how much affection she and her husband had been held.
How kind people were! Regaining her voice, Emily's thanks were
short and very sincere; she dared not trust her voice to say much.
Dropping her eyes, she gazed at the small travelling-clock, with her
name and the inscription in gold lettering embossed on the blue case.
It was lovely. Holding it tightly, she looked up and smiled delightedly.
The opening meet that year had been their first public appearance
after the wedding. In those days, hounds had belonged to her father-
in-law, old Sir Giles, and were kennelled on the estate, in brand new
buildings. One day maybe they would return to the family; anyway
Giles hoped so. He loved hunting and spent a good deal of his free
time with them.

'Hounds, gentlemen – please.'

The master's clear voice rang out, echoing from the walls of the
old house. As if by magic, the ranks fell back and left the way clear
for hounds. Preceded by their master, with Bill and Tom, the whips,
bringing up the rear on either flank, the pack trotted briskly through
the high arch of the gate-house and away down into the park. Directly
behind them rode Giles on Rustler, dancing this morning and snatching
at his bit, eager to be off, restrained only by Giles' gentle hands. On
either side of their brother, two expectant faces looked radiantly ahead
through their horses' ears. Anne's horse was a dark brown five-year-
old she had named Magic. She was a small mare, no more than fifteen-
two; but what she lacked in inches, she more than made up in speed
and ability. Mary's horse on the other hand was well over sixteen
hands; a dark bay with black points and a star, which had earned him
his name. He was seven, and today had thrown caution to the wind
and was enjoying a hearty buck on the springy turf in the park. Behind
them came the rest of the vast field, all wondering what the day would
hold.

The country was well fenced and called for a good horse, capable
of both jumping and staying, and able to gallop uphill and down; that
is if you were to see the end of a hunt with the Ravensworth. They

still carried their old name, and hunted much the same country as they had done in the days of the Regency, when they were first founded.

This morning, following an age-old custom, they drew the home coverts first. Slowly the minutes ticked by. All was silent within. Not a whimper. Not a sound. Giles strained his ears to catch the first whimper. The waiting seemed interminable as he sat at the covertside. Surely, after all his care, they would not draw blank. Rustler, standing now like a statue, flicked his neat ears, first forwards and then back, then forwards again. He was quivering now in every muscle. Giles shifted in his saddle, and instinctively shortened his reins. A crackle in the undergrowth made his horse snort. Looking down, Giles found himself staring straight into two beady eyes surveying the scenery beyond the covert. Then, one by one, hounds started to give tongue within the covert, diffident at first, with nothing more than an odd whimper or two. Scent, evidently, was tricky. Then at last came that wonderful sound as the whole pack got on the line. The crash of music ringing through the covert was too much for Charlie, and he slipped quickly through the bracken and out into the open park. Giles held his breath, and counted twenty slowly. Eighteen – nineteen – twenty. He was well away. Good luck to the little red robber! Giles' 'view holla' ranged through the covert. Hardly had the holla died away on the wind, than the whole pack poured out. Quickly they settled to the line. A blanket would have covered them all.

Round the end of the covert cantered Bill, while over the 'tiger-trap' came the Master, blowing away his hounds. Giles only waited for them both to get clear, before following. Away to his right, he could see the rest of the field tearing down towards the pack. He had been lucky, and got a good start. Rustler, feeling his head free, stretched out his neck and snatched at his bit. Ahead lay the first wall, a hunt jump, reinforced by rails along the top on either side. It was solid. Giles soon realized he had little hope of steadying his horse; his only hope lay in balancing it to the best of his ability. Seeing the two horses sweeping away up the far hill, with the pack another field away to the left, Rustler lengthened his stride and took off. How he cleared the wall and remained on his feet was a mystery. He rapped the bar on the take-off side, hard with his hind legs, faltered, and then galloped on, unharmed. Giles gave a dry laugh.

'Well, boy, I hope that's taught you a lesson!' Patting the dripping neck stretched out in front of him, Giles smiled to himself as they strode on up the hill. White foam, flying back on the wind, bespattered them. The heat was now on, the pace fast and furious, over one of the best stretches of country in the land.

'Gosh! That was a near one, wasn't it?' called Mary, as she galloped up alongside her brother, a few fences further on.

'I guess so. What have you been up to?' Giles glanced at his young sister's mud spattered back.

'Oh, that! I took a toss at the "tiger-trap" after the wall. It was nothing. Seen Anne?' panted Mary, 'I last saw her going well. Magic is proving rather a dear. This is rather green. He doesn't seem to know what solid fences are. But he'll learn!' Mary was the happy go lucky type.

Another quarter of an hour, and hounds checked. Considerable thinning out had taken place during that run. The pace had been too hot for many of the field, and the stiff fences had taken their toll very quickly. It was no day for those who liked to potter about from covert to covert. Out in the open today, there was a screaming scent.

Sheep had been the cause of hounds checking. On the wind-swept 'banks' of the Cotswolds, sheep throve, and nearly every farm had a flock of some kind; Giles himself had a registered flock of Cluns, which ran in the park. Casting, the Master failed to pick up the line. The scent was getting cold and had been badly foiled by the large flock that had bunched into the corner by the wall. Every now and again a hound would own to it, only to lose it again straight away. It was an old hound, Wimbush, who eventually picked up the line and started to speak. With head held high, she wandered up and down the wall, every now and again standing on her hind legs and questing along the top. Halting, she jumped up onto the wall, walked a few yards down it and jumped off into the next field. Casting wide, she gave tongue and then, fitfully at first, she spoke. Within seconds the pack were over the wall and beside her, while the Master rode up and down on the far side encouraging his hounds. With a crash of music, they found again and were away, slowly at first, and then, as the line became stronger, they began to race once more.

Anne had joined her brother and sister soon after they had checked, and this time was close beside them as they galloped down the steep hill and prepared to jump the wall at the bottom. She was thrilled to bits with her new hunter, and felt the glow of happiness and satisfaction that comes with achieving something one has waited for for a long time. This would certainly be a day to remember, as they flew through the vale and up over the banks. Fence followed fence. They were experiencing the real thrill of a good hunt on their own hunters, and the wonderful feeling as a horse rises for its fences, kicks back, and gallops on, only to repeat it a few moments later.

Chapter IV

As the last of the field moved off from the gravel, through the gate-house tower, Maud and Emily, still clutching her treasured clock, made their way to the sweeping lawns on the southern side of the house. From here they could watch the first draw, for the home coverts lay about a quarter of a mile from the house, across the river towards the home farm.

Emily's eyes grew misty as she looked out over the familiar scene. Her mind, though, was not in the present, but away back in the past, back in the days when she herself would have been out, taking her rightful place among the other riders. For two pins she would throw caution to the wind and hunt again herself. In those days, the large stable yard had been full. The Towers had been noted for their hunters and hacks, carriage horses and cobs, all sleek and shining, with a legion of grooms to care for them. Old Sir Giles had prided himself, quite justifiably, on his horse-flesh, and was accounted a notable whip and horseman. His horses had been his pride and joy. Charles, too, had inherited his father's gift to a great extent, though he was never quite in the same class.

'Emily, what is it?' Maud's voice broke through her day-dream, and brought her back to the present with a jerk.

'Nothing really. I was just thinking, thinking of the past like a silly old woman.' Emily blew her sharp nose defiantly and subconsciously straightened her shoulders. 'Come on in, it's cold out here, and they've gone now.'

'Yes. They've gone. I often thought of Ravensworth, its house and its hounds. But I never thought to see them again.'

'Well, you have, even if they have altered considerably. But come, we've not yet had time to talk. I want to hear your news, and I expect you would like to hear ours. After all, it's fifty years odd since we've last seen or heard from you. There's a good deal you may be able to help us clear up and straighten out at long last. Heavens only knows, we've searched enough to find you. Then out of the blue, in you blow. Fate must have sent you. If you wait a minute, I'll just ask Mrs Moss to send up coffee to our own room. We'll be undisturbed there until the others come back. The place will be quiet, so we'd better make the most of it. Morpeth will answer any calls or enquiries.'

A blissful peace descended over the house, as they entered by way of a side-door. Out in the pantry, the clink of glasses met their ears, and overhead the hum of the carpet cleaner, but these were faint and would not penetrate their quarters much, after the hubbub of the previous hour or so.

Away in their own wing, a bright fire greeted the old ladies and bade them welcome to its warmth. With purpose, Emily shut the door and pulled an armchair closer to the blaze for Maud, before pulling up another for herself, on the opposite side. Between them, on a small table, sat a tray. Mrs Moss, good soul that she was, had brought it straight up, only stopping to bank the fire before leaving the room warm and cheerful.

'My, Emily, this is fine and cosy.' Maud settled herself comfortably in a chintz covered chair. In this low ceilinged wing, Emily had used chintzes in all the rooms. In this, and her own bedroom, blue was the predominating colour, though this had a blue that was more grey than blue, whereas her own room had one that was the palest of pale blues, an enchanting colour that suited the old lady's character. The other rooms had their distinguishing hallmarks of colour. Giles' room had a background of rust-red, Anne's one of pale green, and Mary's pale yellow, nearly fawn. The patterns on all the fabrics were the same for the curtains, giving uniformity without monotony. In the main part of the house, Emily had stuck to old fashioned fabrics and colours in keeping with the age of the house and its furnishings. Down in the hall, the grandfather clock struck noon. Over the mantelpiece hung a water-colour. Emily smiled; Maud was peering at it through her lorgnette.

'Well?' Maud screwed up her eyes, as is the custom of many old ladies of failing sight, and ignoring her sister-in-law's query, went on gazing at it in rapt silence. 'Recognize it?' Emily was rather proud of the painting, as well as fond. It had been an unexpected extra wedding present from the members of the hunt, and depicted her and her husband at the opening meet of 1899, with the house in the background and their families grouped round them on either side of the happy couple, with hounds waiting expectantly at the horses' feet. In those days, Emily had been extremely elegant. A tall, striking woman, she sat her horse well, as straight as a ram-rod; so different from the present day ladies who perch, crooked and twisted, on their saddles, to bump all day in the wake of hounds. Admittedly, there were still just a few who could really ride side-saddle, but they were few and far between and nearly all of the older generation like Emily. Her horse had been grey, and against its light coat, her dark habit had stood out, showing them both off to the best advantage. John, at her side, bestrode a fine, handsome black, both horses their wedding present from the hunt. Together the two looked happy and contented, as well they might.

Maud gave a sigh, and let her lorgnette slip from her gnarled fingers.

'My, those were the days. Now, I must know exactly, right from the beginning, what has happened to every one of you, since James and I left. Emily, please tell me, at least try. After all, this is the reason I've come home. Ever since James died last year, I have felt restless. As long as I had him, I was content. We prospered well. Father had been generous, and had given us sufficient to pay off James' debts as well as buy land in America. Even after buying land, we had money enough to build a nice house. Before long, we were doing well; it was the making of James. Away from London, he was a different person. He was young, and by the time we had reached the new land, he had recovered from the effects of his previous life. I myself was happier than I had been since our wedding. As the years passed, we moved to bigger and better parts, till we found the place we really liked and settled there, building up our estate and making friends among the other settlers. Our only regret was we had no son.'

This made Emily prick up her ears, but she remained silent, keeping her own counsel, for there would be time enough later to discuss that.

'Our only daughter, Emma, grew up out there on our estate. You see, we sold our others; and just went on buying new ones till we found the one on which we wished to settle ourselves. Eventually, Emma married the son of one of our neighbours. They in turn took their own section of land, reclaimed it, and built their own house and reared a family. I've eight grandchildren out there now.'

There was pride in Maud's voice as she spoke, but behind it lay a wistfulness that she could not quite hide. After a pause in which she took a biscuit and crumbled it into small fragments, without eating it, Maud continued.

'The snag to that marriage was Augustus. He was proud and conceited, with far too high an opinion of himself. He would come down to Ravensworth Folly, the name which James had bestowed on each of his estates in turn.'

Emily smiled. How typical of James, banished from home, to christen his homes in the New World with a name like that! She wondered what his father would have thought, if he had ever discovered.

'And,' she continued, 'picked up faults everywhere, antagonizing the estate workers and making them discontented. Then when they wished to leave us, he would take them on himself. In this way, he gathered an excellent staff at our expense. Before long, James and Augustus were at open war. With Emma siding with her husband, they slowly drifted away, till in the end we never saw them. It was a pity, but what could we do? His own parents were treated the same. Luckily, their estate formed the western boundary of the country, and was situated some twenty miles from us and his own parents, near another township. So the families never met or crossed in public, except on rare occasions.'

When her sister-in-law stopped, Emily looked up from her contemplation of the fire and asked, 'Do you never see your daughter or grandchildren?'

Maud shook her head sadly.

'No, not now. I did see them once. They all came over for the wedding of Augustus' sister, two years ago, and brought the children with them. This is the only time we've seen them. Augustus refused to let them come when their grandfather was dying. When I decided to come back to England, I merely wrote and told her that, as she couldn't be bothered to attend her father's funeral, I had sold the estate and was leaving for England.'

A knock sounded at the door.

'Come in.'

There was a shuffle outside the door, a clink of a tray, followed by the turning of the door handle, and Mrs Moss entered bearing with her a tray laden with dishes.

'Excuse me, Ma'am, but I thought as how, seeing Master Giles and his sisters are away hunting, you and Mrs James would prefer your lunch up here in the warm.'

'How kind of you! Thank you. Yes, we would prefer it here. I hadn't realized how late it was.' Emily busied herself pulling out a small round table from the wall and putting it before the fire with its flaps up. On it she spread a clean white cloth from the chest near the door on which stood innumerable photographs of the family. Five minutes later, the sound of Mrs Moss's carpet slippers were heard receding along the passage and down the stairs, leaving the two old ladies to enjoy their meal in peace. With the dining-room nearly empty, Mrs Moss had cooked her mistress a special meal as a treat. She enjoyed being left in charge of the kitchens; it gave her a sense of ownership.

With the arrival of lunch, Maud and Emily abandoned the past and reverted to the present. It was impossible to eat and recall the old days at the same time. Their lunch was too delicious to treat lightly, Mrs Moss had done them proud; she loved to make a fuss of Emily and rarely had the chance.

'Well, Emily, now that we've finished that excellent meal and kind Mrs Moss has removed our tray kitchenwards, how about telling me your story and Ravensworth's; right from the beginning, mind!'

Emily remained silent and busied herself with banking up the fire from the rush basket of logs standing beside the hearth, till its blaze had reached a comfortable height. Sinking down into her chair opposite Maud, Emily closed her eyes and lay back, letting her mind and thoughts drift backwards over the many years since she had first come to the Dower House in the village as a small girl. Then, as if by magic, she found herself once more a child.

Chapter V

'Emily, my pet, Sir Giles has very kindly bidden you to the Towers this afternoon.'

'Oh, Mama, do you really mean it?' Emily, a small, dark eyed, slightly wistful child, gazed eagerly up at her mother, who was seated at her escritoire in the window, penning a letter. A graceful lady, blessed with a strong character and features to match, she nodded at her daughter. There was nothing weak about Mrs Stapleford; some found her rather downright manner a little disconcerting to start with, but on further acquaintance, they found an alluring charm and kindness lurking behind her twinkling dark eyes and her rather slow smile which won her many unexpected friends.

It was to this lady's dressing-room that her small daughter had been summoned from her school-room. For the last six months, the Staplefords had been residing at the Dower House on the Ravensworth Estate. An attractive house, built of Cotswold stone with a stone tiled roof, it was situated beyond the village of Ravensworth, on the edge of the park, looking away across a spinney to the river beyond. They had grown to love its quiet and peace.

Until now, the Staplefords' acquaintance with the Towers had not included the children, so it was with great excitement that Emily looked forward to the afternoon. By sight, she knew the family well, for every Sunday, Sir Giles would take his place in the family pews of the old Norman church where they went to worship in the village, attended by some of his numerous progeny. There was Charles, the eldest, a serious, dark haired young man of five and twenty summers. Rather shorter than was fashionable, he walked with a slight limp,

32

and unlike his next brother, James, he detested London and town life. This may have had its roots in his limp, but whatever had sowed the original seed, he preferred the life of the country. His time was spent running, very ably too, the estate for his ageing widower father, and hunting and fishing according to the season, and this, together with shooting, filled his days. The sport in his native Cotswolds was good. The River Raven was not noted for its fishing but was tolerable, and Charles was blessed with many friends, and the rivers of Herefordshire and Wales were well within his reach. James, on the other hand, just down from Oxford, was already proving something of an embarrassment to his father, though only twenty-one. Ever since going up to Oxford, he had run into trouble; now his life on the Town was not improving matters. Every time he came home, he was once more in debt. Gaming of all kinds held an unanswerable fascination for him; offer him a bet, and he would take it regardless, always with the same drastic results. Even so, it was hard not to forgive this tall, fair youth, with his engaging smile. He just liked a good time and, being handsome, he readily achieved it. Between Charles and James came their eldest sister, Anne. She too, was rarely seen nowadays, for she, two years younger than Charles, had been married nearly four years and lived some ten miles distance from the Towers to the west. She had married Edward Horton, Squire Horton's only son and heir. They had a small estate of their own and were very happy, with a growing family. Harriet, who came next to James, was twenty. She was still at home; but would shortly be getting married too. Emily had taken an instant liking to Harriet, with her sharp face, a contrast to Anne's round one, and her sparkling eyes. One Sunday, when Emily had dropped her collection during the rather lengthy sermon, Harriet had looked across at the little girl and winked. On either side of her were the two younger Ravensworths, Mary, a delicate little girl of thirteen, and Sarah, who looked the elder of the two, but who was, in fact, the youngest, being only a year older than Emily herself. These two were to become the dearest friends of nine-year-old Emily. Between the two little girls and Harriet came John, who was up at Oxford, the youngest and gayest of the Ravensworth boys. James' high spirits led him to excess; John expended his on sport of all kinds.

Lady Ravensworth's demise had come some nine years earlier, following the birth of the youngest and last of the Ravensworths, leaving a growing family to the tender care of old Nanny and a doting aunt, Sir Giles' sister Julia. For years she had resided with Sir Giles and his family, so the passing of Lady Ravensworth had only left a sad gap, but caused no lasting upheaval within the household.

Aunt Julia, sewing in the long sunny window of the drawing-room overlooking the park, first perceived little Emily and her governess, coming up through the park by way of the path that skirted the shrubbery, on its way to the front door. She looked even smaller than usual, with a frailness born of many years in India. As she walked, her long ringlets, confined by a pale blue ribbon, bobbed on her shoulders, while a straw bonnet becomingly framed her pale face. Peeping below her frock were two spindly legs encased to the calves in white kid boots buttoned up the sides, the intervening space being filled by a pair of black stockings. Rising from her chair, Aunt Julia put down her needlework and proceeded sedately through the hall, her long skirts swishing the floor as she moved, in good time to see Buttermere open the front door.

'Good afternoon, Miss. Will you come in, please?' Stepping back, he gave a small, stiff bow.

'Thank you.' Emily stole a shy glance up into the stately face of the butler hovering above her. Dropping her eyes from his face, she turned to her governess, waiting at her elbow, 'Thank you, Miss Dinmore, for bringing me. I'll be all right now.' Emily's voice had an odd seriousness, that sounded peculiar in a child so young, not unlike her mother's, till one realized she had been reared in India until a year ago, when she had returned, on the retirement of her father, Colonel Duncan Stapleford, with her parents. At first she had felt lost and bewildered in England, but slowly she was growing accustomed to the new life, and found much of interest in the woods and park. The countryside was proving a fund of excitement.

'Come on in, my child. I am so glad your mother said you could come.' Emily looked quickly round to see where the deep, resonant voice had come from. In the shadows by the grandfather clock, she noticed a diminutive old lady watching her through a raised lorgnette.

34

She was tiny, but very dainty in her tight waisted frock, with its long sweeping skirts. What Miss Ravensworth lacked in inches, she made up for in dignity. Seeing the child's bewildered face looking shyly across at her, she dropped her lorgnette and held out both hands in welcome: swiftly crossing the intervening floor, she bent and kissed the child. Turning to Buttermere, she said briskly, 'I'll take Miss Emily to join the school-room party myself. Where are they, please?'

'Miss Naughton took Miss Mary and Miss Sarah for a walk, Ma'am; but I believe Miss Harriet has just returned from a drive with Master John. I will send word to them, if you would so desire, Ma'am.'

'Please do; and ask Miss Harriet to come to me in the long drawing-room; thank you. Come, my child, we will wait for the others there. Miss Naughton is inclined to get slightly carried away on nature rambles, and forgets the time!'

Emily gave a little giggle; then checked herself hastily, looking up under her long curling lashes. Aunt Julia turned, and smiled down at the child, whose hand still rested in hers. She was a kind woman, devoted to her nephews and nieces. Unlike her sister-in-law, their mother, who had been easily bored by her large family and longed for the bright lights of London and the whirl of society life, Aunt Julia had never asked for more than to be allowed to remain at her beloved Ravensworth, with her family. For three whole seasons she had endured the rigours of Society. How long they seemed, and how thankful she had been when at last they came to an end and she could return home! Emily perched on the edge of a hard chair, with her small feet pressed tightly together, obediently and politely answered innumerable questions.

After what seemed like eternity, the quick footfall of a young girl was heard coming along the small hall towards the doorway.

'So sorry to keep you waiting, Aunt Julia. Shall I take Emily with me? I saw Miss Naughton coming up from the lake with the children. We could go and meet them, for I see they have the trap out.' Turning to Emily, she held out her hand. 'Come, we'll go and find them. If we're quick, you could have a ride in the trap.'

Emily slid from the chair and curtsied to Miss Ravensworth, before placing her small hand in Harriet's outstretched one.

Soon she was chatting happily to the older girl. Harriet had a gift, a rare and valuable gift, of putting people at their ease, and to Emily, she was something new and rare. Going out of the house by way of a side-door, Harriet and Emily came on the school-room party bowling gaily into the yard at a smart pace.

'Hallo, Harriet; is that Emily?' Sarah was standing perilously in the trap, waving excitedly. 'Look, we've caught a newt and a frog!' The small girl flung open the little door of the governess cart and bounced out. With a ready smile, not unlike her brother James', she came across to her sister and Emily.

'Well, so you've come back at last. Aunt has been looking for you. A nice way to treat a guest!' Harriet squeezed the small hand still in hers and winked. Cutting off Emily's stuttered protests. 'Who's coming with me? I'm about to take Emily for a drive round the park.'

'Me!' chorused the little girls, jumping around excitedly.

'Well, Miss Harriet,' Miss Naughton paused, looking at Mary, 'I think—'

'Yes, maybe,' responded Harriet quickly, 'Mary, darling, would you mind helping Miss Naughton as tea is nearly ready; we won't be long.'

Mary stood still, her blue eyes looking too big for her pale, thin face. She blinked and turned away. Emily was shocked. She knew Mary was delicate, but being young the truth had not dawned on her until Harriet spoke. Harriet's dealing with her small sister had been kind and gentle. Quietly, she put her arm round the thin shoulders that shook with suppressed sobs.

'Mary, my pet, don't cry. You've done enough for today; you're tired. Tomorrow, I will take you out myself, and maybe, if he's free, John will come too. You would like that, wouldn't you?' Mary sniffed and nodded her head, before turning away to follow their governess into the house with a dragging step.

'Poor Mary,' Sarah remarked when she had gone, 'there's so little she can do. You would never think that until her illness, she was as strong as any of us.'

Once clear of the rear gates that led into a small lane, hemmed in by stone walls, Harriet turned the small, tubby pony between the shafts, towards the home farm. At first he was disgruntled, and refused to leave the prospects of a warm stable and an evening meal.

'Oh, he's always doing this,' remarked Sarah cheerfully, watching Harriet persuading the pony to go on. With a flick of his tiny ears and a shake of his shaggy mane, he gave in with some semblance of good grace, and trotting smartly, set off along the lane. Emily was enchanted with her drive and sat very still and erect beside the gay Sarah, who never stopped chattering. There was nothing shy about this freckled child, with happy blue eyes that shone in her small face, framed by long fair hair. Even the rakish angle of her tammy was in keeping with her character.

'Harriet, please.' Sarah looked pleadingly at her sister and held out her small, brown hands for the reins.

'Well—' Harriet looked down at her sister with a quizzical look, and then winked at Emily, 'Why should I?'

'Please.'

'What does Emily say?'

'Oh, please, let her, Miss Ravensworth.'

'All right, but don't take Bunny too fast. Promise.' Harriet held out the reins and Sarah, shifting nearer to her sister, took them.

'Thank you.' Once the reins were in Sarah's hands she became silent, and she did not speak again until the farm was reached.

Tying Bunny to a ring in the wall, Harriet led the children towards the buildings, casting a quick glance at Emily's white kid boots. Not quite the right wear for a farm, but the weather had been dry and the yard was fairly clean. Sarah ran here and there, dragging Emily by the hand. Knowing the farm well, she was intent on showing it to her new friend. This was the first time Emily had been to a farm and she trotted gaily after the bigger girl. It was a hive of attractions – calves, baby pigs, chicks – not to mention the bigger animals like the cows which were being milked in a long shed, and the cart horses stamping in their stable. Harriet watched for a few minutes and then went up to the farmhouse to see Mrs Stow. Returning ten minutes later, she retrieved the children and drove them back to the house. Bunny was willing to start this time, and halfway home Harriet handed the reins to Emily. At first Emily was frightened, then once she found Bunny would go along at his own pace, she gained confidence and turned, her small face aglow with pleasure, to Harriet.

'Like it?' Emily merely nodded. Her voice had vanished, for she was too happy to speak. Until now, her only experience of driving had been behind a coachman in a coach with Mama. Very different from what she was doing now.

There was just time to have a quick look round the stables on their return. Sarah took Emily from box to box, telling her all their names, while Joe hovered in the background. He had been head groom at the Towers for many years and had known all the family since his boyhood, having been born and bred on the estate. He had entered the stables as a young lad and under the eagle eye of his father, who had been head groom before him, had worked his way up to his present position.

'Goodnight, Joe,' Sarah waved as she led the way across the yard in the wake of her elder sister. 'Thank you for showing us the horses.'

'Goodnight, Miss Sarah, Miss Emily.' Joe was fond of children and had given all the young Ravensworths their first riding lessons.

Up in the school-room, Sarah and Emily found Miss Naughton and Mary awaiting tea. Over tea, Emily soon found her natural shyness vanishing; it would have been hard to resist the welcoming friendship of the two youngest Ravensworths. Their spontaneous friendliness had been extended from the moment of their meeting, and no one could remain shy for long in that atmosphere. Oddly enough, Emily had found herself slipping effortlessly into their games and chatterings, even though it was all very new to her. Her life, until now, had been a solitary one, bounded on all sides by convention, for in India, there had been no other children of her own age. How she welcomed the change that their return to England had wrought. At first, neither Mary, now resting on a couch, nor the more boisterous Sarah could understand or realize that Emily's life had been so very different from theirs.

Between playing games, the three small girls discussed their different lives. While the two Ravensworths told Emily of their life in England, she regaled them in her turn with stories of her own life in India, her journey home, almost a year ago, to an England she had never seen and her life in London, where they had had a rented house near Hyde Park, then her joy, when her parents, finding the life of London too isolated for their taste, had moved down to Ravensworth. Now they lived in the country and visited the metropolis only at rare intervals. For Emily, the move had been a release, for London had soon begun to pall and threatened to become as constricting to a small girl as India had been.

Dusk was falling when Miss Dinmore arrived to escort her small charge home through the park. It was a reluctant Emily who bade farewell to her new found friends and followed the maid down to the drawing room, at Aunt Julia's request. Quietly she stood, while the maid who had come for her announced her presence to her mistress.

'Oh, there you are, my child. Come in! Thank you Aggie.' Aunt Julia held out her hands in welcome. 'I want you to meet my brother and eldest nephew. Harriet, of course, you've already met.'

Glancing across to the large window, Emily was glad to see Harriet sitting there, catching the last of the daylight for her neat stitches. A gifted needlewoman, she was enjoying her task of making her trousseau.

'Good evening, sir.' Emily gave a gulp and a small curtsy to the old man seated in a deep armchair by the fire. She had seen him many times, but beyond patting her one day on the head as he passed some remark about her to her parents, Emily had never made his acquaintance.

'Enjoy your drive and visit to the farm?' he asked, watching her pale face from under beetling brows. His voice was soft and kind.

'Yes, thank you, sir.' Enthusiasm strengthened her voice.

'Good! Ride?'

Emily merely shook her head.

'Well, well, must see about that. Goodnight, my dear, come again soon.'

Harriet rose and escorted her small friend to her governess, who was waiting for her charge in the hall. Saying goodbye, she bent and kissed the child.

Chapter VI

The Ravensworths were true to their word, and before long Emily found herself bidden again to the Towers. The small Ravensworths in their turn came to tea at the Dower House, driven there in Bunny's trap, for Mary could no longer walk far. These autumn days were halcyon days for Emily, who was rapidly coming out of her shell and blossoming into a different child. Her parents watched this transformation with a mixture of relief and gratitude. Emily's long years in India had made her old beyond her years, and she was slowly learning to race and play with Sarah across the broad acres of the park. But much of her time she spent with Mary, helping her to find some flower for her collection, or just playing some quiet game, while Sarah went out with her elder sister. Sarah would have stayed, but Aunt Julia liked her to have some outlet for her energy, which was impossible when she was with Mary. Whenever she could, Aunt Julie would remain with Mary, and Emily would join Sarah and Harriet for long drives through the countryside. She loved these and eagerly looked forward to them.

The autumn days gave way to winter, and with the turning of the leaves, the park took on a new look, a look of expectation for what was to come. All the woods were a-glow with copper coloured leaves and ripening holly berries, while all the blackberries had long since come and gone, with other autumn fruit. The corn had been harvested and now the fields were gradually turning from their golden stubble to the rich brown of new turned plough. Jack Frost, too, had not been idle. His fine pictures were to be found on the windows early in the mornings, while down in the park, every blade of grass suspended a tiny, fragile cobweb. To Sarah and Emily, these were the work of the pixies who they believed lived in a hollow willow by the lakeside. Their childish fantasies found full rein during their games in and around the old house, and they were never happier than when they were lost in their own world of make believe, a world to which Mary and Sarah readily admitted Emily, shortly after their first meeting.

With the approach of winter, few days passed without the children meeting either at the Towers or the Dower House, though during this time Mary's condition deteriorated considerably. For many days at a time, she would remain indoors, seldom venturing out. She was content just to lie quietly in Aunt Julia's dressing room, resting on a couch by the fire. These latter days were sad days for all, and Emily and Sarah spent more and more of their time together out of doors.

Coming into the house one day shortly before Christmas, Emily made her accustomed way along the wide landing to Aunt Julia's dressing room. Gently, she turned the handle and pushed the door open just enough to slide in. Closing the door behind her, she stood and waited till her eyes became accustomed to the faint light, for the room was lit only by a single night-light and the dancing flames of the fire. Looking across the room, Emily saw her little friend dozing quietly in the firelight.

'Mary.' Emily crossed on tip-toe over the carpet and sat down on a tiny needlework stool beside the fire, near the couch, looking up anxiously into the pale face resting on the pillows. 'Mary, I've brought you these stamps. Papa had them this morning from India. They're new.'

'Thank you, Emily.' Mary's voice came with effort. Her limp hands remained where they were under the rug that covered her thin body. She made no move to take the precious stamps, which a week or two earlier would have sent her into transports. Foreign stamps were rare, and Emily's contribution to Mary's collection had greatly added to it, much to the envy of her other small friends who were sent into raptures over some of the rarer, more colourful stamps.

A soft movement at the door made Emily turn her head, but still she sat on in the firelight. How long she had been there, she knew not. She had just sat. Harriet crossed to the silently shaking figure by the fire and slipped her arm round her shoulders, gently lifting her to her feet and leading her from the room. Outside the landing was deserted.

'Come, my dear, Mary's tired today. Don't cry.' Harriet's gentle voice only caused Emily to cling to the older girl and weep copiously. 'Hush, my dear, don't upset yourself. She's not in any pain.' By this time they had reached Harriet's own room. Pushing open the door, Harriet led the weeping Emily in and closed the door. Crossing to the bell-pull, she rang for her maid. 'We'll wait here awhile, I think, and get Betty to bring you some warm milk and biscuits. Then you will feel more the thing. I'm going to ask my brother, then, to drive you home. As you know, Sarah has gone to spend a few days with our sister Anne. We didn't expect you today. What brought you?'

Emily's sobs were ceasing now. The brighter lights and warm comfort of Harriet's presence were taking their effect. Emily began to feel safe once more. In with Mary, she had been frightened and bewildered, and an odd sadness had crept over her that she couldn't explain.

'I'm sorry. I was alone. Mama and Papa had gone out to call on someone. Miss Dinmore was busy with her needlework. So I thought, as it was a nice fine afternoon, I would walk up through the park and bring Mary some new stamps that came for Papa this morning. I left a note for Mama, as Miss Dinmore had told me to go out and play,' there was a slight note of defiance in Emily's voice, 'and then left by way of the garden gate, coming up over the foot-path from our house to here.' Emily gave a sniff and a stifled sob.

'That was very sweet of you. I'm sure she's delighted; but she didn't sleep much last night. In the morning, she'll be brighter again, so don't worry.' Emily knew as well as Harriet that that was unlikely, though this was Emily's first encounter with a dying person. Something had told her this afternoon that her small friend, whom she had grown to love dearly, would never get better. Her days were numbered. How long she had, no one knew, least of all Emily. Even so, she was glad and grateful for Harriet's kindness and reassurance.

'Oh, there you are, John. Is Aunt in yet?' Harriet was seated at her writing table in the window, when her brother's brief knock sounded on her door, some twenty minutes later.

'Yes, she's in with Mary now.' John smiled kindly at Emily, still sitting by the fire.

'Thanks, I'll go to her then.' Rising from her writing table, Harriet crossed over to Emily and bent down with her arm round the little girl, as she spoke to her gently. 'John will take you home. Be a good girl and go with him. I'll see you again soon, never fear. I'll come down to the Dower House.' Standing close to the two girls, John held out his strong hands to Emily, and helped her to her feet. 'And John.'

'Yes.'

'Would you please give this note to Mrs Stapleford?'

'Certainly. Come, Emily, my dear, my horses are waiting.' Together the tall lad and the small girl left the room and passed down the stairs to the side-door and out into the night where, true to his word, John's pair of greys stood harnessed to his curricle, with a groom at their heads. At any other time, Emily would have been delighted at the prospect of a drive through the park with John, but to-night she was too sad. She felt as if a load of lead had descended on her shoulders, crushing her beneath its weight. The drive was short, and throughout, Emily sat motionless, slumped under the rug with which John had covered his small passenger. Every now and again he could feel a sob shake her slender body. Removing one hand from the reins, John drew the little girl closer to his side, wrapping the rug tighter round her thin shoulders.

By the time the Dover House was reached, Emily had drifted into the slumber of the exhausted, so handing his horses to the Staplefords' groom, John jumped down and lifted Emily in his strong arms. Anxious parents clustered round, and Emily was carried off to bed, where her mother tucked her in and kissed her good-night.

It was the last time Emily ever saw her small friend, for Mary died quietly in her sleep a few days later. Over the once gay Towers, a gloom settled. Mary had been loved by all. A kind, thoughtful girl, she had endeared herself to everyone who knew her. A gentle child, she had accepted her long illness with fortitude and courage. Clever beyond her years, she had delighted in reading, devouring book after book, always thirsting for more – a contrast to her younger sister, who had little or no time for reading, or for that matter learning, and was only really happy when she was out of doors.

Emily saw little of Ravensworth during the next few weeks. Confined to bed with a chill, she had not even the pleasure of meeting the Ravensworths at church, though Harriet, true to her word, visited her once or twice bringing her fruit from their glasshouses. Up at the Towers, the family were in deep mourning. Harriet's wedding, planned for January, was postponed indefinitely. In the stables the hunters stood idle, and in the coverts the game-birds were left undisturbed.

Christmas drew nearer and nearer. Already the choir were practising the Christmas hymns in the village church, under the watchful eye of the vicar. On still nights, the strains of well known carols drifted on the night air to the Towers. Sarah, at home again, was oddly silent. She was alone. Years younger than her other brothers and sisters, she felt deserted. She no longer had anyone to play and laugh with.

Meeting his daughter one day walking aimlessly through the park, kicking at the tufts of grass with the toe of her boots, Sir Giles stopped. Normally, he troubled himself very little with his growing family. But Mary's recent death had upset him deeply, and the sight of his youngest daughter's face, pale and strained above her black frock, shocked him.

'Why, Sarah, my child, what's the matter?' He patted her shoulder kindly. Sarah, too miserable and unhappy, remained silent. Her silence spoke more than any words could have done. Taking her hand, her father led her off towards the kennels to visit his hounds. The old man and young girl made an odd contrast, Sir Giles looking old enough to be her grandfather rather than her father, having aged considerably following the loss of his wife. Every afternoon about this time, Sir Giles would be seen making his way through the park, a ritual built up over many years as Master. This unexpected treat cheered Sarah, and by the time she left she was, for the first time in her life, on easy terms with her father, whom till now she had loved and respected from afar.

'Well, my dear,' her father was the first to break the silence that had fallen over them on leaving the kennels to walk back, 'I've been thinking. How would it be if I were to ask dear Mrs Stapleford if you could spend Christmas with them? I am afraid parties are out of the question here, but with Emily, under her mother's wing, you could go to a few given by your closest friends.'

'Oh, Papa, could I really?' Sarah looked wistfully up into her father's face. A kind face, surmounted by pure white hair; and a pair of grey-green eyes that twinkled beneath beetling brows, which returned her gaze. 'Thank you.'

Two days later, on Christmas Eve, as the snow blew in flurries across the Cotswolds, heralding the advent of further snows to come, Sarah drove with her eldest brother Charles away from the Towers. As they set off from the house, the chill air stung Sarah's cheeks, whipping some colour back into them, and she drew the rug closer round her legs. The lights of the village shone out across the park as they descended the hill to the church; glittering forth from the unshuttered windows, they offered a welcome to the small girl, eagerly straining towards seeing her friend. In all the cottage windows Christmas decorations glowed brightly and cheerfully. How pretty they had made their small homes and how cosy and inviting! Sarah almost wished she could see inside. Here and there the shutters were being drawn, and outside the night air became colder. It would be a white Christmas. Being a notable whip, Charles covered the three-quarters of a mile to the village at a brisk trot. Reaching the village outskirts, he drew rein and drove slowly up the long winding road towards the far end where the Dower House was situated, and swinging in at the gates, dropped his horses to a walk.

Up in the school-room window, Emily knelt with her nose pressed to the cold panes, counting the snowflakes as they fell. She could hardly suppress her excitement. Then up the lane the carriage lamps shone out in the dusk, and the sound of eight hooves reached the small girl in the window. Hardly waiting to see Charles' two magnificent chestnuts swing into the drive, Emily slid from the window seat and ran to the door. Far below in the hall, voices floated up to listening ears. Her mother, emerging from the drawing-room, looked up and beckoned to her small daughter, as she spoke.

'Emily, my pet, come down. Sarah is here.' With flying feet, Emily flew down the double flight of stairs and danced across the hall. 'What a clatter!'

'Sorry, Mama.' Emily dropped her head in repentance, and then looking up, grinned with pleasure at Sarah. 'I am so happy you've come.' Emily's grin was infectious; Sarah's face broke into smiles, and she returned her friend's ardent embrace.

Sarah stayed at the Dower House well into the New Year. Soon, she and Emily had settled into a happy routine under the vigilant eye of Miss Dinmore, and they found the past drifting away. The weather grew steadily colder, and down in the park, the lake froze over and the deer came right up to the house to be fed. At the end of January, Charles drove the children over to Anne's home. This proved a happy move, for no longer were they on their own. Anne had a hopeful family. So far they numbered three. Guy, the eldest, nearing his third birthday, was an independent, sturdy lad, who bid fair to resembling his father Edward, a tall, dark haired man in his thirty-third year, and blessed with a will of his own. Robert came next, a golden haired toddler of eighteen months. Emily was enchanted with them, and would spend hours playing in the nursery or with their baby sister Jane, who had been born about the time of Emily's first visit to the Towers.

With the coming of spring, the children returned to their own homes. A few days later Miss Ravensworth's carriage was seen coming up the lane to the Dower House. Emily was sitting at the time with her mother.

'Oh! Mama!' The little girl scrambled up into the window-seat to see better.

'Emily, come down.' Her Mama spoke sharply. 'Really, you must learn to behave, or I won't have you in here.'

'But Mama, Miss Ravensworth is coming.'

The drawing-room door opened, revealing the sombre little figure of Miss Ravensworth. In her mourning, Aunt Julia looked even smaller than usual. Formalities dispensed with, Emily, much to her disappointment, left the room.

Miss Ravensworth settled herself on the sofa and looked earnestly at her hostess. Those eyes were the eyes of the troubled.

'Mrs Stapleford, forgive my coming; but my brother and I have a great favour to ask you and your husband. So I'll come straight to the point. The trouble is our little Sarah. Since Mary's death, she has been extremely lonely, and before Christmas the solitude began to tell on her. This was offset by her long visit to you and then to Anne; she recovered her spirits slightly and started to forget before she came home. Unfortunately, the Towers has brought it all back to her, her sorrow and loneliness, and she is miserable, though she tries bravely not to show it. It is because of this that my brother and I wondered if you and your husband, dear Mrs Stapleford, would consider letting your Emily come to us during the day. Then the two little girls could share a governess and be companions for one another. My brother says the choice of governess will be yours entirely, and we would send a carriage every morning to fetch Emily and return her in the evening. In this way you would still see your daughter and not be cut off from her in any way. If you could agree, you would be doing Sarah the greatest kindness in the world.'

Talk continued for a while in the drawing-room, and then Miss Ravensworth took her leave. Emily, peering through the window panes of her school-room, watched her go and ran to the stairs in the hope of being allowed to return to the drawing-room and her mother's side. She waited eagerly for the summons that would send her flying down the stairs again. With Miss Dinmore away, she had not long to wait, for her mother felt it her duty to have her with her.

'Emily, my pet, we're going out for a drive; please put your coat on.' Emily danced off to do as she was bid. No doubt, in time, she would learn of the purpose of Miss Ravensworth's visit. Grown-ups could be very trying at times!

Chapter VII

Before the week was out, a routine had begun that was to continue for many years. Colonel Stapleford, hearing of the proposal from his wife later that night, after Emily was safely in bed, had readily agreed to their granting the Ravensworths' wish.

'You know, my dear, it will be a very good thing if Emily goes to join Sarah at the Towers. She's been alone too long. Sarah will do her good, and she's already benefited from Sarah's companionship. We will send a note up in the morning. Which governess do you wish for, my love? It is up to you?'

'Oh, Duncan, I'm so glad you agree. I am delighted at the suggestion. I see no reason why some days Sarah shouldn't come down here for a change. As for the governess, I'm in favour of Miss Naughton.'

Emily had to contain her curiosity over Miss Ravensworth's visit to her mother until the following morning. At first she was delighted, then her face dropped.

'But Mama, will I never live at home again? I mean, will I become a Ravensworth?' Her anxious face puckered up.

'No, my pet, why should you? Now, don't cry.' Mrs Stapleford put her arm round her small daughter's shoulders and kissed her. 'Come on, don't be such a goose.' Leading Emily to a couch, Mrs Stapleford sat down and drawing Emily down beside her, explained the whole proposal. Emily listened, wide eyed and open mouthed, then as her mother finished, she gave a funny gurgle of laughter and put her arms round her mother's neck.

'Oh, then, I think I will go. How soon can I start, please?' Emily's

48

eyes were dry now and shone with glee. 'And how soon will Miss Dinmore leave?' She stole a sideways glance up at her mother.

'You unnatural girl! We haven't decided yet, she comes back today from her mother's. Anyway, it might be a good idea to keep her on to care for you in the evenings!' Mrs Stapleford smiled quizzically at her daughter, whose whole face was a perfect picture of horror.

'But, Mama!—' Emily gave a strangled gasp.

'And why not, Miss?' Emily bit her lip and held her counsel. 'As a matter of fact, Miss Dinmore is leaving anyway at the end of the month. Mrs Horton wishes for a governess to take charge of Guy, and Miss Dinmore will be excellent, as she prefers small children and loved little Guy. She is delighted at the prospect of being back with a small family. Now you will have a maid to look after you, and Miss Naughton is going to teach you and Sarah. She is accustomed to teaching older girls and has been at the Towers since Charles was small and has taught all the children. Papa and I were going to get you another governess, but now there is no need, thanks to kind Miss Ravensworth. Happy at the arrangement?'

'Thank you, Mama, it will be much nicer sharing with Sarah. Miss Naughton is so nice and kind and does not fuss like Miss Dinmore.' Mrs Stapleford smiled. She knew Emily had found the constant vigilance of Miss Dinmore rather overpowering and was glad that such an excellent solution had offered itself. Some would say that she took her daughter's wishes too much into account in such important matters but Mrs Stapleford preferred it so.

Soon, both Sir Giles' daughter and Colonel Stapleford's were experiencing the hidden joys of close companionship. Promptly, every week-day at nine o'clock, the Ravensworths' coachman would call for Emily, only to return her again in the evening at six o'clock. On Sundays, after church, Sarah would come to the Dower House for the day, or they would drive over to Anne's. Emily loved her drives to the Towers and looked forward eagerly to them. Lessons, too, took on a new meaning for both girls. No longer were they working only for themselves; now they had each other to compete against. It was much more fun. Sarah, to her father's and aunt's relief, was no longer content to let her lessons slide, but at long last was taking an interest in learning. With her elder sister Mary, she had been content to let the elder girl do all the work, and had seen no disgrace in being behind. Now the tables were turned. No longer the youngest, she was determined to keep ahead of Emily, who was clever into the bargain. This friendly rivalry added to the pleasure of sharing their activities.

Even during the holidays, the arrangement continued, though their time was spent out of doors or playing together. For some time now, both girls had, under the strict eye of old Joe, been learning the rudiments of riding, assisted by the long suffering Bunny, who was more suited to his small trap. He was extremely fat and at times bone lazy. For a long time, Sarah had longed for a pony of her own. While Mary had been ill, it had been out of the question, but now the wish was even stronger, and secretly, so it was with Emily, who loved animals.

At last the day of Sarah's birthday dawned. It was still nearly dark when Emily, slipping out of bed, scrambled to the window and pulling back the chintz curtains, she peeped out. Across the wide expanse of park, a haze hung like a cloud. It was going to be fine. Dressing quickly, Emily scampered down to the hall. She was joining Sarah for breakfast this morning, as a special treat. Hardly had Emily jumped down from the trap than the door was flung open and Sarah rushed out.

'Come on, Emily, you're late.'

'No, she's not. It's you who are impatient.' John held out his hand to the younger girl.

'Yes, she is.' Sarah, bright eyed and flushed with excitement, hopped up and down, her fair hair bouncing on her shoulders. Excitedly, she embraced her friend.

'This young Miss would wait for you, and now says you're late! So shall we proceed now and have breakfast later?' Sir Giles placed a hand on either child's shoulder and led them through the east door. His face wore a genial smile. He spent more time now in the children's company, and of late had been taking them with him on his rounds of the estate. Their tracks though this morning were turned towards the stables, where they were met by Joe Lydd.

'Good morning, Sir, Miss Harriet, Master John, Miss Emily, Miss

Sarah, happy birthday, Miss!' The old man permitted himself to smile, and led the way into the long airy stables. All along one side were rows of boxes, while on the other were roomy stalls. It was to this side of the stables that Joe led the party, right to the far end. As they passed down the boxes, welcoming whinnies rang out, though the stables were only a quarter full. The remainder awaited the return of the hunters, who were enjoying a well earned summer's rest in the park. Now both little girls noticed something new. On the last two stalls, two doors had been fixed, turning them into boxes. Excitement mounted in Sarah's heart. Could it be? Joe moved forward and unlatched the first door, and stepping back, ushered the family forwards. His face wore an odd smile, but he never lost his dignity.

'Sarah, happy birthday, my pet!' Sir Giles pushed his youngest towards the open door. Sarah stood rooted to the spot, unable to believe either her ears or her eyes.

'Papa!'

Strong hands lifted her and carried her through the door, into the box.

'There, goose, now do you believe it?' John's soft voice came from a long way off. Sarah was lost in a trance. Then it broke and she flew towards her present, standing at the back of its box facing the door. The small brown pony surveyed the proceedings with a calm, dark eye and an intelligent expression. In the middle of her little head, a tiny star shone out.

'Oh! You darling!' Sarah hugged her possession, paying no heed to the others, for her face was buried in the thick black mane. Her dream of years had come true.

'Emily, my dear, let's leave Sarah to enjoy her new companion. Yours is still waiting for you.' As Sir Giles spoke, Joe opened the next box to reveal to Emily's startled gaze a replica of the first, save that in place of the star a half-moon graced its pretty head. Emily was almost speechless and found herself stammering excited thanks. After all, it was not her birthday!

'Well, well, still in a trance, my dears.' Aunt Julia had come to fetch her family into breakfast. 'You must come now. You can see them again, but if you don't hurry you will be late for your ride!'

Autumn brought a pleasant change to the Towers. At last out of mourning, the estate went gay for Harriet's wedding. She was to be married in style in the old church in the village, and the reception was being held at the Towers.

The big moment had at last arrived. Inside, the church was full, while near the altar rails, David waited for his bride. Outside, Harriet, attended by six small bridesmaids led by Sarah and Emily, suffered the last adjustments to her long flowing veil, a family heirloom. She looked dignified and calm as she took her father's arm for the long walk up the aisle. Dressed all in white, with a magnificent bouquet of late roses ranging from deep gold to the palest of pale yellow, she entered the church and started on her journey into marriage.

As they stood behind Harriet at the altar rails, listening to the service progressing towards the climax, Emily began to let her eyes and mind wander, oh so slightly, but enough to start her wondering. How odd and strange it all seemed! It was her first wedding and she was enjoying herself. One day, she too might be standing there, in Harriet's place. She was going to miss Harriet, miss her terribly. It was a pity she was going to live so far away. David's home lay in Sussex near the Downs, where his family had lived for generations.

During the last few months, the little girls had grown fond of David. He had spent a good deal of his time with them in Gloucestershire. An old school friend of Charles, he had been welcome at the Towers for a number of years now, having first paid a visit one Christmas for the hunting. Harriet's ready sense of humour and quiet good looks had soon captivated him, and in turn, David found favour with the newly presented Harriet. Throughout that season, they had met frequently, and as often as he could contrive, he had come down to the Towers. Soon, various Mamas were nodding their heads and speculating freely. They were to be disappointed. Two more seasons elapsed before David sought out Sir Giles in his study, and begged his permission to marry his second daughter. This had been readily forthcoming, for David found favour in the eyes of his future father-in-law and Sir Giles had been delighted. So too, had Aunt Julia, who had always been fond of David and fostered his friendship with her niece. Excitement had been rife when the news of Harriet's impending marriage the following January had been made known to the rest of the family. But their joy was to be short lived, for hard on the heels of their rejoicing came their shattering loss of little Mary, which drove all other thoughts from their minds.

Emily's wandering thoughts came sharply back to the present, with Harriet's clear, strong voice giving her responses. Before Emily realized what was happening, the ceremony was over. Harriet and David Lavenham were man and wife and they were all moving slowly towards the vestry for the signing of the register. Emily glanced down at her white dress with its pale gold sash and matching shoes, for with each step her toes peeped out beneath her hem. Out of the corner of her eye, she could just see Sarah's toes as she walked and wondered what she was thinking about.

The days that followed Harriet's wedding were soon back to normal. At the Towers her presence was sadly missed, for she had spent much of her time in the company of the little girls, taking them for drives and picnics and arranging many other things that delighted them.

Even the grand wedding was eclipsed in the eyes of Sarah and Emily with the arrival of October. Neither girl could sleep that night. Instead of going home, Emily spent the night at the Towers. Tomorrow, they were going cubbing. Without protest, they went to bed early, after Sir Giles had promised they could ride over to the meet with him. It was arranged for a cross-roads a few miles beyond kennels, so it meant an early start.

Tumbling out of bed at four-thirty, they rubbed the sleep from their eyes and hurriedly donned their habits, fidgeting while Martha helped them fasten the tiresome bits.

'Do be still, please, Miss Sarah.'

'Sorry, but be quick, please!'

Soon, free from Martha's administrations, both girls were skipping gleefully downstairs.

'Good morning, Papa.' Sarah reached up and kissed her father before falling into step behind him. Together they went out of the east door. Charles and John were already out in the stable yard, waiting for them. For Emily, the early morning held a special magic fascination. No birds were yet awake, and the trees stood out black and sinister against the early morning sky. Soon, the five horses' hoofs rang out on the cobbled yard. Slowly they moved away from the stables and down the back drive. Five minutes later, Emily felt a tingle of happiness run up and down her spine, as they reached the kennels to find hounds and the hunt staff waiting for them; twenty minutes more, and the cross-roads came in sight on the crest of the next hill.

Away in the village, the church clock chimed out six, its loud peal floating up the long valley to the waiting horses, and as the last chime died away on the stiff breeze, hounds moved off at the heels of Sir Giles' hunter. An air of expectancy ran through the hounds and communicated itself to the small girls on their ponies. It was exciting. Beneath her, Emily knew she had a true friend and companion. Nutmeg's tiny ears flicked backwards and forwards.

'Good pony.' Emily patted the woolly neck in front of her and glanced across at Sarah on Star. They were well suited, and standing with a far-away expression on their faces. This Emily knew to be misleading; Sarah, like herself, was just blissfully happy.

Sir Giles, as usual, was hunting his own hounds, so John took charge of the young entry and guided their steps and initiated them in the art of hound-work. Though there were no exciting long runs of anything special by which to mark their first morning's cubbing, the small girls could not have enjoyed themselves more. There would be time and enough for good runs later in the season, and cubbing had its own thrill. By the time the sun had risen in the late autumn sky, turning it a fiery orange and setting the hills alight with its reflection, they had turned their horses' heads for home. Sir Giles was no believer in staying out once the morning was advanced. In almost complete silence they rode over the banks and dropped down into the valley that would bring them to the drive from the south gate that ran up past the lake to the gate-house tower, a well loved landmark. Only when they were safely in the house and eating a large and welcome breakfast, did the small girls start to chatter; then it seemed as if they would never stop! Such had been their delight.

Time heals, and by the time that Harriet's hopeful family had increased by two small daughters and they had firm hopes that their wish for a son might soon be realized, Mary's death had faded into the background. Though her memory would live forever, her name no longer brought tears to their eyes.

David, knowing his father-in-law's delight at seeing his many grandchildren, saw to it that they travelled into Gloucestershire to see him at frequent intervals. Sarah and Emily looked forward to Harriet's coming and would plan for days ahead when they knew she was on her way. Aunt Julia, too, welcomed these visits from her niece and her tiny children. The Towers was never happier than when it was full. Not only did Harriet return to her own home, but Sarah and Emily paid many visits to her in Sussex as the years went by, spending as much as a month at a time.

Early in the summer, Sarah and Emily returned from a six weeks visit to Harriet to find James at home again. This was a rare occurrence, for James preferred the dizzy life of London to that of the country, and seldom spent more than a day or two there. Their hopes of seeing something of him during the coming weeks were soon shattered. For, though he remained in residence at the Towers, they saw little of him. James was dancing attendance on an acquaintance of his childhood, an extremely pretty young girl whom he had had the good fortune to meet again during her first season. A chance invitation had brought them together after several years. Her tall willowy form, elegantly dressed in a becoming gown, was set off by her dark hair piled high on top of her head. James, coming late into the vast room, had cast his eyes round in hope of seeing some of his friends. Instantly, they had alighted on this vision and thereafter, he had had eyes for her and her alone.

Before the season was out, James had presented himself at her papa's London home and requested Sir Christopher Rudgely for the hand of his daughter. Sir Christopher, being well acquainted with the Ravensworths, having lived some ten miles to the east of the Towers for many years, was reluctant to give his consent to the match. Maud was young yet, and there was time enough before she need think of marrying. But his wife was ambitious. After all, as she explained to her long suffering husband, Sir Giles Ravensworth was no longer a young man, and Charles had long since become the despair of matchmaking mamas who had hunted him unmercifully for years, determined to catch him for their aspiring daughters, so James, one day, would inherit the vast estate of Ravensworth with its wide and prosperous acres, not to mention a title that was far older, though, she hastened to add, no more honourable, than their own. So it was that his objections to the match were overruled, and an engagement announced.

If the announcement came as a surprise to those at Ravensworth, it was no less welcome. Maud was liked by all the family and they gladly accepted her into their midst. James had made a wise choice, if marry he must.

James had been home for some weeks when his father summoned him to his study, one bright afternoon in late July. Outside, the bees hummed in the borders, buzzing their way busily from bloom to bloom among the well-filled beds. Aunt Julia had a passion for flowers; her garden was always bright with them and their fragrant scent filled all the rooms. Through the open windows the song of the birds drifted soft and sweet. Since his return, James had expected this summons, and had hoped it might never come, though it was odd that his father had made no mention of his pending marriage.

'Better to, James.' Anne was at home, staying for a few days with her family. She often brought them over to see their grandfather. This summer, she had been several times, enjoying the leisurely peace of the park at this time of year.

'What, face the music? What's he going to say?' James made a face and rose to his feet from the bench beneath the massive tree that stood at one end of the lawn.

The interview that followed was something James would remember for a long time. The study was situated on the shady side of the house, and as James entered, his father was busy reading a document and failed to look up or intimate that he knew of his presence. Slowly the minutes ticked away. Would his father never finish? He shifted sightly from foot to foot, and twiddled his fingers behind his back.

'Well, my boy?' Sir Giles' voice made his son jump, for his eyes were still on the document. 'What's this?' He tapped at the paper with his forefinger impatiently. 'Who said you were getting married and what on, I would like to know? Tell me that?' James shifted uneasily. The last time he was at home, he was in debt. This time it was even worse. Besides, he knew Sir Christopher wished for a handsome settlement as well. 'Now, boy, come on? How much this time?'

James ran his tongue round his dry lips.

'Six – six thousand, sir.'

Silence followed. Sir Giles looked his son up and down with a cool eye.

'And you calmly plan to marry Miss Rudgely?'

'Yes sir.' James looked his father straight in the eyes. He was used to these interviews now, though this one was the worst of any so far. They had taken place regularly ever since his days at Oxford and James was hardened to them.

'I see. Well, as Sir Christopher has been fool enough to give his consent and accept you for his daughter, I shall have to comply with the terms of his marriage settlement.' He tapped the document with his finger as he spoke. 'But let me tell you this. It will be the last time I settle your debts for you. I will do it this time and make the required settlement, but mind you, it is the last, and next time you go abroad, wife or no wife! Understand?' Sir Giles' eyes snapped.

'Yes, sir. Thank you.' James backed hurriedly out of the room and went in search of his sister Anne. He had always turned to Anne when he had been in trouble, and now he felt he must talk to someone who might understand.

Autumn was upon them, and down on the home farm, the corn was ripe and stood in long, neat rows of stooks, awaiting the carts to carry them to big barns for storage. It was a wonderful sight as the mist rose over the stubble in the mornings, shrouding the hills in a thin, light blanket of cloud. These autumn days were bliss to the two young girls, rapidly growing into womanhood. Only that summer, they had been given two small hunters to replace their outgrown ponies, Star and Nutmeg, who, at Sarah and Emily's request, had been given to Anne's growing family. Shadow and Bess were eminently suited to their job. Standing about fifteen hands, they combined plain commonsense with good looks and conformation, having a strong cross of pony blood in their veins. Though sad at parting with the ponies that had taught them so much in the last four years, Sarah and Emily soon found the added advantage of riding larger ponies, and now looked forward to the coming season with eagerness.

The wedding was smaller this time, and took place at the Rudgelys' home in late September. Maud's darkness was a contrast to the fairness of James, and her wedding dress was beautiful. The long train fell to the ground behind her and was carried by two small pages – Anne's sons. As soon as the wedding was over, the young couple left for London. This was the last the Towers was to see of them except at rare intervals, when they chose to visit the Cotswolds.

Chapter VIII

James' downfall came two years later with the celebrations for the Diamond Jubilee of dear Queen Victoria, whose long and successful reign was being marked on 22nd June in the year of Our Lord eighteen hundred and ninety seven, with due respect and rejoicing throughout her lands. In Ravensworth, tucked away in the Cotswold hills of north Gloucestershire, the village was en fête for the occasion. High on the hill that rose steeply behind the Towers, a huge bonfire crowned the summit. As night fell, the village would climb to its side and a light would be put to the vast pile. Like a thousand others throughout the land, it would flare up to the heavens, proclaiming her subjects' loyalty and love.

The June morning was still very young, as Sarah and Emily rode out through the estate with John. It was a glorious morning, with an air of expectancy everywhere. Visiting the many tenants on the estate, they found the same spirit prevailing; the old Queen's subjects were waiting to pay homage. Leaving the park, they turned up the lane that led to the Dower House and shortly afterwards, overtook Emily's father, just returning from the village.

'Well, well, who have we here? Nice to see you, my dears. Come on up to the house and have some refreshments.' Colonel Stapleford's smile was welcoming as he spoke. A tall, lean man, he was still remarkably erect for his advancing years. As of old, he still sported a moustache and the Norfolk jacket of a few years earlier, with a deer-stalker hat, which had found instant favour with him, as well as Sir Giles. Emily, now she was emerging into womanhood, bore a strong resemblance to her father, for though he was now grey, she had the same rather mousey hair that he had had as a young man, and the same facial features. Walking up the long twisting drive beside her father, the likeness struck John very forcibly. Even at a distance, it was unmistakable. Only their voices were different; Emily had inherited her mother's. The true likeness, though, was hard to define. John thought it lay in a certain movement of the face muscles when they laughed. Emily would screw up her face in an odd way and her eyes had a deep set twinkle that lurked in their dark depths.

They were greeted at the house by Mrs Stapleford who, hearing horses, had come down the shallow steps from the front door to meet them. She was a pleasure to watch, for she moved with perfect co-ordination – the mark of true grace and dignity. Embracing both girls warmly, she shook John by the hand.

'Well, my dears, how nice; come on in. Dear John, would you be very kind and take the horses round to the stables first, please, and then join us in the drawing-room for refreshments.'

'Certainly. The pleasure's mine.' John took the proffered reins and vanished round the corner of the house.

Ushering Sarah and Emily into the cool of the hall, she went on,

'How lucky, I was just on my way to gather flowers, but they can wait. I like to pick my own. So much nicer.'

These visits were a common occurrence between the two families these days and they were on very easy terms.

'Sir, my father asked me to enquire if you and Mrs Stapleford would care to be taken up in one of our carriages, to-night. It would save taking out your own horses. There are five going from the Towers, so there would be plenty of room. We thought Emily could come with Sarah and me in my curricle, my sisters and James will be going in their own, taking their families, while my father and aunt would be delighted with your company.' John looked first at Colonel Stapleford and then at his wife, waiting for their answer.

'That is extremely kind and thoughtful of them. How about it, my love?'

'But, by all means. Would you please thank Sir Giles and Miss Ravensworth on our behalf, and say we would be delighted. No doubt, we'll be seeing them at the fête this afternoon and can then thank them personally.'

'They will look forward to seeing you, I know.' John smiled down at Mrs Stapleford; he had grown fond of the old lady over the years and enjoyed coming to see her.

They chatted for a while, then rode home through the village. The Dower House lay at the opposite end of the village to the vicarage. As they clattered down the road, their hooves echoing off the cottages, their horses made quite a noise. Hearing the sound of horses, Agnes ran to the vicarage gate to greet them. A rather plain child, a year or two younger than Sarah and Emily, she sometimes came to tea at the Towers. Nearly always these meetings were strained, for Agnes was extremely prim and her freckled face showed acute disgust. If anything but the stupidest games were suggested, and Sarah seldom accepted these games with good grace, she would usually provoke Agnes into a huff, just for the devil of it.

'John, go on,' urged Sarah at his elbow.

'Why?' He turned in surprise.

'We'll never get away – she's silly.'

'Hush! She'll hear you.'

Emily, catching these heartfelt utterances and exchanges between brother and sister, gave a little smile to herself, and knowing her mount's dislike of being tickled behind the girth, dropped her whip hand with its long slender cane and swept Bess's side, oh so gently! Like lightning, in a frenzy, the bay mare shot forwards with a plunge and raced headlong down the road. Emily laughed to herself. They galloped past the big oak, standing majestically in the centre of the road, the old coaching inn, the Three Bells and the picturesque village pond of ducking fame, and swinging left she made for the park.

John, flabbergasted at the spectacle of his friend's flight, swiftly gathered his own mount together and followed with Sarah, calling his apologies and excuses over his shoulder to Agnes, who stood wide mouthed and horrified by the gate.

Entering the park, they were met a few seconds later by an impish grin and a pair of sparkling, laughing eyes.

'Well – satisfied, Sarah?'

John looked sharply at Emily.

'What do you mean? What happened to Bess?'

'Why? – nothing – '

Simultaneously the truth dawned on her companions, and throwing back their heads they roared with laughter, nearly doubled up in their saddles.

'You'll catch it, if ever Papa hears of it; and hear they will! The whole village was watching,' replied Sarah wiping her eyes with the back of her hand.

'What of it?' Emily tossed her curls and cantered off, calling over her shoulder, 'I'll say Bess was stung!'

John raised his eyebrows, ventured to say something and then, thinking better of it, shrugged his shoulders. What use was it anyway? Emily always managed to have the last word!

The afternoon proved an unrivalled success all round, one of the novelties being a bicycle race for the men of the parish. For some years now, bicycles had been in vogue among the younger generation at the Towers, so amid much laughter and chaffing, Charles, James and John joined in the fun with gay abandon.

Unknown to his brothers, James had been in recent contact with one of his cronies who lived in the neighbourhood. Hardly had they met than bets were being laid on the outcome of the race. Harmless enough in itself, but as usual with James, it never stopped there. He could never say no to himself. Throughout the previous week, before leaving London, he had been involved with some friends and once again was well and truly under the hatches. Now he saw a hope of recouping his serious losses, and making a bit besides. Henry, Maud's brother, was his worst influence, and shortly before lunch, as they returned to the house, this rakish young gentleman was to be seen riding through the park. Maud, staying at the Towers, encountering her brother, was none too pleased; for where Henry lurked, trouble was seldom far behind.

That night, waiting in the shadows on top of the hill for the big fire to go up, Henry made his way stealthily round the backs of the many carriages and carts lined up on the outer fringes of the gathering, towards the far side where he had spotted the Ravensworth contingent, with James' carriage slightly apart from the rest. Maud, hearing footsteps, was the first to spot her brother. She frowned, then spoke lightly.

'Hallo, brother. What brings you here? Thought you had gone home after that fiasco this afternoon.' There was a note of caution in her voice that Henry could sense a mile off.

'Well, I haven't – James, I want a word with you, please.' Henry jerked his head towards the rear of the gathering.

'No. Not now!' snapped James.

Maud was puzzled; she had sensed trouble all afternoon, but she never questioned either her brother's or her husband's movements. Even so, she began to feel sick with fear. Henry paid no heed to James' denial and persisted. He was a hard headed young man and could not be won over by James' ready smile; there was something rather sinister about his dark features and grim, twisted smile. James waved him impatiently away and moved his vehicle nearer to his family, in the hopes of precluding any further conversation. He might have saved himself the trouble, for Henry was not deterred as easily as that. Sir Giles, unseen by his son, had been an interested spectator of this interchange, and was worried. He had never cared for Henry Rudgely or his influence on his younger brother-in-law. Fond of his erring son, Sir Giles was still a man of his word. For a time all had seemed well and the young couple happy and contented. That Maud and James loved each other, Sir Giles never doubted for a moment. But whether their love was strong enough to guide James' footsteps onto a safer and steadier plain, Sir Giles knew not; only time could tell. This latest encounter with Henry bore no good. Something was wrong, Sir Giles thought sadly, the weight of the truth weighing heavily on his heart, for he knew the reason. For two whole years since the day of his marriage James had never asked for another penny. It was a sad and bitter blow to the old man, for he knew his duty.

When darkness settled on the waiting crowds, as far as the eye could see, beacons started to glow, and slowly their glorious, fiery red flames crept high into the star studded sky. To the west, the mountains of Wales proclaimed their allegiance to their queen; to the south, the long line of the rolling Marlborough Downs and the far distant hills of Somerset; while closer at hand the Devil's Chimney on the prominent hills beyond Cheltenham, blazed out in 'Honour and Glory' for the old Queen's long and prosperous reign.

James' ultimate sailing for the New World with Maud came as a terrible shock to everyone at the Towers. They had been unaware of the depths of the conflict between father and son, and at first it was hard to believe. It had all been too beastly, brought to a head by Maud's own brother. She had felt responsible, and James, bitter against everyone, especially his father, had left in a towering passion of injustice. That had been many months ago, and now their names were never uttered, save in the privacy of their own rooms, and as the time for launching Sarah and Emily into 'Polite Society' drew near, James and Maud were seldom mentioned. By rights, Sarah should have been a Jubilee debutante, but Emily was too young; so with her usual kindness, Aunt Julia had capitulated and Sarah's coming out postponed a year.

Sarah, to her doting aunt's disappointment, had grown far larger than was pleasing in a young girl. Unlike Emily, she was big boned, and appeared at first sight to be even bigger than she was. As a child, her long fair hair that hung limply on her shoulders had never mattered; now, refusing all efforts to make it curl, it was a constant worry, for piled high, as the fashion decreed, it only went to accentuate her height. In contrast, Emily was more fortunate, for she was also tall, but slightly built, and her long hair curled naturally round her sharp face, falling in cascades down her back. In another week, they would all leave for London. Both girls were wildly excited and could talk of nothing else. For weeks now, great parcels had been arriving from Cheltenham and London, containing such exciting things as new gowns and other things to divert a young girl's mind.

Emily's recollections of London were dim but nevertheless there, but for Sarah, the country mouse, the whole place held a wonderful fascination of depths unplumbed. Before the Season was more than a few weeks old, Emily's presence was eagerly looked for and she never lacked for partners, for she was bright and gay and had a ready wit. Sarah, on the other hand, was less fortunate. Her forthright tongue failed to find favour with the mamas of hopeful daughters, even if her partners found her conversation refreshing after the insipid small talk of the other girls. After the first excitement of seeing new places had worn off, Sarah found herself bitterly disillusioned and London life stuffy and restricting, and soon longed for the country again.

An unexpected pleasure awaited the two girls in London. For some years now John had been in the Army and the Towers had seen little of him. Shortly after joining his regiment, he had been posted overseas, only returning in time for the Jubilee Celebrations. Now stationed in London John, resplendent in his regimentals, was soon a familiar sight in the Park, riding with his sister and her friend, much to the consternation of Emily's many admirers. They made a striking trio, for they all rode well and Sarah was at her best on a horse. His presence in London during the Season was extremely opportune and acceptable. As the weeks passed, Emily found herself looking for the familiar figure and fretted if he was detained. This new feeling for John had begun on his return at the time of the celebrations; until then he had been Sarah's brother and a dear companion whom she had taken for granted during the ten years she had known him. He had been gay and light hearted and ready to join in any fun that might offer itself. During their enforced separation, Sarah and Emily had grown from children into young women, and the transformation had been completed in his absence, so that he had returned to find two different people outwardly, but not inwardly.

Coming late into a crowded room one night, bright with lights and fabulous gowns, John cast a swift look round the swirling dancers. First Sarah whirled past him and waved. Then on the far side of the room he spotted Emily, resplendent in a gown of pale golden yellow, with yards and yards of lace and leg-of-mutton sleeves. She was dancing with a fat, podgy, young man, with a moustache that rose and fell as he talked. All of a sudden a sharp pang of jealousy swept through him. In two swift strides, he was across the floor and at Emily's side as the music stopped.

'Thank you, sir – Miss Stapleford.' John bowed low, and then offered his arm. Before Emily could protest, even if she had so wished, she found herself whisked away, with only time for a brief word of thanks to her late partner, who merely gaped, open mouthed, at the retreating couple. 'Dear Emily! I must talk to you; where can we go?' John's voice was urgent as they made their way across the floor towards a small room leading off the main one. 'This will do; sit down, then we can talk in peace.'

Emily shivered slightly. For weeks now she had had eyes for no one save her childhood friend, and longed with all her heart for the moment when he would speak. To her disappointment, at first they talked only of trivial matters, then, nearly desperate with love, Emily burst out.

'Oh, John! When are we going home? Please, I can't stand much more of London – not at present.'

John was startled; he had been just talking about their plans for Christmas at Ravensworth.

'Why, Emily, what's the matter? You're trembling. Come, do tell me. Aren't you happy?' Casting his eyes quickly round to see they were alone, he slipped his arm round her slim shoulders and drew her close, kissing her curls that tickled his face. Gently hugging her, he went on, 'Emily, darling, it's all right, we'll be home soon. Only a week now. You and Sarah are going down on Monday and I'll be down on Christmas Eve. So don't fret, my darling, I shan't forget you. I could never do that.'

Chapter IX

Darkness had fallen by the time the Ravensworth party drew up at the familiar front door and stepped down onto the gravel to be greeted by old Buttermere. To everyone's delight they found Harriet had preceded them with her family and was waiting in the hall. Anne, too, would be home in time for Christmas itself. Emily's reunion with the Towers was brief. Hugging Sarah and Harriet, she jumped back into the coach and with a rumble it swung away through the arch that led to the back drive and set off towards the village and the Dower House. Her heart was singing with joy. The heavy clouds, hanging grey and menacing, passed unnoticed as they rounded the lodge into the village and were greeted by the welcoming lights in the cottage windows. Outside, the north wind howled and threatened snow, as it swept down over Stow-on-the-Wold. Like the Towers, a reception party awaited Emily's arrival. Her parents, who had travelled down with Aunt Julia, had arrived before her, and were partaking of tea in the drawing-room. Never had it smelt so good, or a fire looked so welcoming as the log one that greeted her. Stripping off her gloves joyfully, she laid them on the table. Her eyes shone. She was home. In a day or two, John too would be down and they would be reunited.

Early the next morning, Emily rode up through the park to visit Sir Giles. She found him reading a long letter in his study. He laid this down, picked up another, then looking up he smiled at his young visitor. Dressed in a blue habit with a fetching hat, she looked older and more composed than she had done before she had left to begin her first season.

'Why, Emily, this is nice. Come on in, my dear. Sarah has been telling me all about your season.' The old man's eyes twinkled, then dropped again to the second letter. With a slight frown, he tapped it with a slightly gnarled finger. 'Got another grand-daughter!'

Emily longed to know more. James must have written to his father, or had Maud's family written? – she would never know. All she hoped was that James had at last written and the old man would now be content. It was sad to see his father. When his name was mentioned, his face took on a far-away wistful look, tempered with remorse.

Returning a couple of days later from a Christmas Eve shopping expedition with her Mama, Emily had the first knowledge of John's return. Coming into the hall, Papa came out of his study and beckoned to his wife, smiling at his daughter as he did so.

'My love, would you spare me a moment, please?'

Emily was agog to know what could possibly be going on behind the closed door. It seemed like hours since they had gone in and shut the door firmly, excluding her. From her seat in the drawing-room, where she had gone to wait for her mother, Emily heard the horses come to the door again; a few minutes later they drove away. Filled with deep curiosity, she hurried upstairs to her room, where the windows gave a good view over the snow covered park. Sure enough, there they went, at a brisk trot up the back drive. What on earth could be up? To while away the time until their return, Emily picked up her needlework and tried to set a few stitches, but soon threw it down again. It was hopeless; she could not concentrate.

For an hour, Emily had to possess her soul in patience, then came the welcome sound of horses once more upon the drive, followed by the sound of the front door being opened to admit her parents. Leaving her room, Emily went swiftly to the head of the stairs and prepared to descend to the lower landing.

'Emily, my pet; oh, there you are,' said her mother, stripping off her muff and going towards the stairs. 'Come on down to my dressing-room, please.'

In silence, Emily walked calmly down the stairs to meet her mother coming up from the hall, while Colonel Stapleford, his part played, retired once more to his study.

Following her mother into her room, Emily shut the door and waited.

'Come, my dear, sit down.' Mrs Stapleford patted the couch beside her and smiled up at her daughter. Emily obediently sank down on the end of the couch, her mind in a whirl of conjecture. She folded her hands in her lap to stop them shaking, clenching them tightly till they turned white at the knuckles.

'Well, my pet. I expect you are wondering why your papa and I have just been up to the Towers. This morning, while we were in Cheltenham, John Ravensworth came to see your papa.'

'Oh!' Emily exclaimed and blushed to the roots of her hair. Her mother raised her eyebrows and looked at her daughter through her lorgnette. It was most unnerving.

'I see,' Mrs Stapleford dropped her lorgnette and her face relaxed. Emily gave an inward sigh of relief. 'It's not unexpected. Well, John's been down and requested Papa's permission to pay his addresses to you. After consulting Sir Giles, we've given him our blessing. We are dining there to-night!'

Emily's mind was in ecstasy. Would to-night never come? With infinite care she dressed herself with aid of her maid, Lucy, choosing from her wardrobe a simple gown of pale blue lace over an undergown of deep sapphire blue which shone through the lace giving it a shimmering appearance as she walked.

Stepping down from the coach in the wake of her parents, Emily felt all of a sudden terribly shy and uncertain of herself. Her last encounter with John had been that night in London. Silently, she followed her parents into the vast hall, her eyes lowered to the floor. Hearing her name she looked up. Aunt Julia's arms were held out to the young girl in welcome.

'Emily, my child.' The little lady stood almost on tip-toe to hug the apparition in blue that met her eyes, Emily had never looked better than she did that night. Her dark eyes were ablaze with fire and her usually pale face glowed with excitement. Her mousey hair hung in becoming ringlets on her slender shoulders confined with a matching ribbon and swept fashionably up at the sides onto the top of her head, giving her dignity and poise. She twisted her fan incessantly, the only sign of her inward turmoil; otherwise she was outwardly calm and composed.

Leaving their elders to enjoy a game of cards in the drawing-room, the younger Ravensworths retired to the hall to dance, the four girls taking it in turns to play the piano. As the evening wore on, Emily's turn came and she moved across to take her seat on the exquisitely worked piano-stool that bore the hallmark of Aunt Julia's needle. John, with a smile, took up his position by her elbow.

'May I?' John bent low over the piano and dropped his voice to little more than a whisper. 'Did your Papa tell you of my visit?' His eyes anxiously sought her face.

The candles in their branched stand threw their flickering light across the ivory keys and alighted on her long slender white fingers as they flew up and down in a waltz. She played impromptu, her heart thumping wildy against her ribs till they ached, and her close fitting gown, she thought, feeling as though it would split or else she would suffocate. For a second or two, she kept her eyes on the keys, then, raising her face, looked shyly up into the one above her. There was no need for words. Neither spoke. Their trance lasted for barely a minute – the dance came to an end and the others came crowding round, oblivious of what had taken place, so close and yet so far from them. In seconds, they were on the floor and dancing to Harriet's nimble fingers.

As they gathered for their departure sometime later, Aunt Julia drew Emily down to her in an embrace.

'Happy, my child?'

'Oh, Aunt Julia, I'm on top of the world!' whispered the girl into the shoulder that enveloped her.

Many hours passed that night before Emily dropped off to sleep. Eventually, worn out, she succumbed to its grasp and the next she knew her maid was waking her on Christmas morning. Though the family were told of the engagement after church on Christmas morning, the official announcement was withheld till both families had returned to London in the New Year, so as to give the young couple time to enjoy their new found happiness together. Even so, the news had preceded them, and the notice in the *Gazette* was almost unnecessary!

The wedding, to take place at Ravensworth, was fixed for October, and at the end of the Season, the two girls returned to the country. Emily was reluctant to leave her John, and would have preferred to remain, but duty called and John would be unable to see his future bride, even if she had remained, so with much misgivings and a heavy heart she took leave of him and accompanied his sister down to the tranquil hills of her native Cotswolds.

The weeks that followed gave Emily little time to miss John. The preparations for her forthcoming wedding were in full swing. Mrs Stapleford spent many hours with Aunt Julia in consultation, for she was a tower of strength, having already married off two nieces and a nephew! She entered into the whole affair with surprising energy, enjoying every minute of it.

The day drew near, and with it the growing alarm of the troubles in South Africa, which worried Emily more than she would care to say. John, her precious John, was on the staff of Lord Roberts and might be called overseas again without notice.

Down in the village, the preparations were nearing completion, and the small church, where eight years before she had stood in wonderment behind Harriet, was once again a smother of flowers. Sir Giles had been responsible for this, having sent them down from the Towers as his special contribution to the wedding. The gardens and succession houses were famous throughout the Cotswolds and all the year round were a profusion of blooms and exotic scents which were a joy to behold. The church looked wonderful.

At last the great day arrived. Emily, resplendent in her white wedding dress with a long veil, walked slowly up the aisle to where John awaited her coming. In her wake followed six small bridesmaids, looking angelic as they came two by two in their long dresses of white embroidered with tiny sprigs of flowers in a multitude of colours. Their small faces were framed with bands of flowers holding back their long flowing hair. First came two three-year-olds, Anne's Bertha and her cousin Helen. As they walked, their wondering eyes sought out the faces of their mothers. Behind them came the terrors of the family, Anne's six-year-old twins, Susan and Mary. Their impish faces grinned as they passed their grandfather. Lastly, with the weight of the other bridesmaids on their consciences, came Jane, who was now nine and her cousin Alice, who was a year younger. It was Emily's regret that Rosemary, Harriet's second daughter, had had to be left out. Poor child, she had broken her leg some weeks before and could not walk yet without help. All the same, she was sitting next to her grandfather and enjoying herself.

Back at the Dower House for the reception, the guests moved freely in the warm sunshine, thanks to the big windows that had been opened for the occasion, giving access to the sweeping lawns from both drawing-room and dining-room, which had been cleared to make way for all the hundreds of guests that thronged to Ravensworth for the wedding. The season had hardly started in London, and the Ravensworths and Staplefords had a wide circle of friends who had journeyed many miles to be present at the event. It was a tremendous success. All the same, Emily and John were thankful when at last they could escape from the heat and noise that surrounded them for several hours.

The happy couple were to be home again for the opening meet on 1st November. In the meantime their peace was shattered by the tragic news of the outbreak of war.

'John, what does this mean?' Emily anxiously held up a copy of the morning paper, a couple of mornings after their wedding. They had travelled into Sussex the day before, Harriet and David having lent them their house while they remained at Ravensworth. It was a sweet house, a small Sussex manor, built about the same time as the Towers and surrounded by a modest park.

'What it says, my darling. The Boers have attacked.' John put out his hand and laid it on his wife's. 'But don't worry, my regiment isn't under orders yet. Maybe it won't last long.'

This was all very well; Emily knew there was danger, and John was only trying to divert her. She was sorry when the time came at last for them to leave and return home. The manor had grown on her and she longed to remain. The peace and solitude just suited her mood. She wanted no one but John.

One of the many wedding presents the young couple received was from the members of the hunt of which Sir Giles was master. It took the unexpected shape of two delightful hunters. John's was a black thoroughbred with a small white star, while for Emily, there was a little grey mare. She stood barely sixteen hands with a good shoulder and a sweet temperament.

The morning of the opening meet broke fine and dry. October had been pleasant and cubbing had gone well in the absence of the young couple. On some days now, Charles carried the horn in place of his father. Sir Giles was getting on in years and slowly was handing more and more over to his son. Charles was well liked and his easy manner enabled him to get on with his tenants, as well as with their neighbours. But the welcome that greeted their father on his appearance on the gravel, warmed the hearts of his family. As long as he lived, Charles had not the least wish to usurp him.

Ten minutes before hounds were due to move off, the family horses were brought to the door and Sir Giles took up his position in front of the house, with John and Emily in the centre and all the rest of both families grouped round. Their healths were drunk, and John thanked the members, on behalf of himself and Emily, for their wonderful present. This was their first public appearance and everyone had come to pay their respects to the young couple. So great was the crowd that hounds were late moving off, an unheard of thing for Sir Giles! Nevertheless, his congenial smile beamed on all. The day that followed was well up to expectations. Drawing the traditional home coverts, a fox was soon a-foot. Before long, a view holla from Charles told them that he had gone away on the far side. Emily was delighted with her new hunter. Well schooled, it jumped well, making little of the stone walls that abounded in the Cotswolds. Galloping by her side, John was equally pleased with his big black. It was hot, but he did not mind. It could jump big, kicking back as it did so. Soon they had drawn away from the majority of the field and were sailing along in the van of the hunt, with hounds running away to their right in a slight arc. Fence after fence they jumped together. How little did they realize that in two months John would be overseas!

Chapter X

The eight eventful years that had passed since Emily and John had ridden so happily over the rolling hills of their beloved Cotswolds, had seen many changes at Ravensworth. They had been years tinged with sadness, for though Sir Giles still reigned supreme, he was a very old man and now nearly blind. To the sorrow of his devoted family, he was failing fast, and waited only for the fulfilment of his most ardent desire, a grandson to carry on the family name. Charles had never married, James no longer wrote – whether he had a son, no one knew; all their hopes rested with John and his young wife, and as the years ticked by their hopes faded. It was Charles who now ran the estate and to whom the tenants and farmers came more and more for help and advice, in the old man's absence; though even Charles was answerable to his father for all he did, and would never have wished it otherwise. As long as the old man breathed, Ravensworth was his and his alone.

The winter following the departure of John for the South African wars plunged the Towers once more into the deepest sorrow and mourning. One terribly bleak and dismal night in mid-January, with the temperature below freezing and all the countryside gripped in winter, Aunt Julia died after several weeks of illness. Sad and shaken, her family mourned her loss. She had been adored, especially by Sarah and Emily, to whom she had been a devoted friend and guardian. Hardly had they recovered from the shock of Aunt Julia's death, than it was followed by another. The day of the funeral had been cold and bleak, with a bitter, biting wind sweeping in off the hills, freezing the black clad figures as they stood lost in sorrow at the grave-side. Within

74

the week, Colonel Stapleford, too, was gone, leaving behind a grieving widow and daughter and many friends who had come to value his friendship and good common-sense. It was a sad household indeed at Ravensworth that winter, for close on their own loss came the news that was to end one of the longest and greatest of all reigns England had ever known. The country was plunged into mourning for the loss of their Queen on 22nd January. So was the New Year of 1901 heralded in.

Emily's mother only survived her father by three years and died peacefully in her sleep one night in early June, plunging the two families once more into mourning. Mrs Stapleford had been liked and admired and her loss was felt over a wide area.

With the new reign came peace and John was able to return home to his wife and family. The years passed steadily and part of their time was spent in London, where they now had a town house, and part at Ravensworth, where Sir Giles had given them the Dower House for their own. These were happy years and the young Ravensworths were content, but never ceased to pray that one day their prayers might be answered. It had been hard on them both, for John's sisters had both had such large and healthy families, and their wait seemed never ending. Then at last, during the summer, it seemed as if their prayers were about to be answered – but would it be a son?

Outside, the first snows of winter were swirling in over the bare hills and settling in a clean white blanket on the countryside. The night was dark, and the snow muffled the night sounds of the outside world. Inside the Dower House, the house was quiet, the deathly quiet of waiting only broken by the steady crackle of the log fires that burnt in the hearths, throwing out a cheerful glow. In the library, John paced up and down impatiently, while from the wall brackets, the candles threw their soft light on his troubled face. Hour after hour, he waited. The chill night was only disturbed by the chiming of the church clock in the village – nine – ten – eleven, then from the floor above, came the first faint cries they had waited for for so long, and thought never to hear. Soon these were followed by louder more lusty cries. Evidently the latest edition to the Ravensworth family had good lungs. To everyone's joy, and especially Emily's, it was a son. Their long wait and Emily's secret despair was at an end. Their prayers had been answered. As for Sir Giles, well, he now had his grandson and heir; he could be content and enjoy his last years in peace.

Hardly had the nurse come to break the glad tidings to John, than he was bounding up the stairs two at a time.

'Darling!'

'Satisfied?' Emily smiled happily up at her husband, standing at the foot of the bed, gazing down at her and their small son, who was tucked up in his cradle beside her bed, sound asleep, a tiny tuft of red hair just showing. He was a Red Ravensworth!

'Yes, darling, more than satisfied. Bless you.' John moved nearer to his wife and bent down to kiss her gently. 'What are we going to call our son? I can't wait to tell Father; he will be overjoyed.'

'John, of course!'

'What, after me?' He laughed, and added with a twinkle, 'Well, then, he had better be Duncan after your father, as well, and we will call him Duncan.'

'All right.' Emily was suddenly tired and with a wan smile closed her eyes and drifted off into a deep sleep. The sleep of the contented. Now she had everything she could wish for in this life: her John, and now, her Duncan. She asked for no more.

Early the next morning, before it was light and the world astir, John rode off through the park to the Towers by light of the moon. It was as if the park was rejoicing with him. Slowly the first light of morning began to break, as dawn came up over the hills, casting a red glow on the glinting whiteness of the fresh snow. John's face, wreathed in smiles and glowing with happiness and pride, reflected the glorious morning. Sensing his master's mood, Black Knight, though getting on in years and only used as a hack now, danced and sidled on the cold ground, leaving an odd pattern through the powdery snow. With a snort, he let off a series of bucks worthy of his younger days.

What did John care? He was feeling reckless, and with a laugh he dropped his hands and let his faithful friend have his head. With a bound, the big black shot forwards.

'All right, old boy; buck away; I don't care. This is the greatest day since my wedding and your arrival. Come on, let's gallop.' Together, they swept over the ground towards his old home, his heart beating joyously against his ribs and his breath coming in puffs, cut off by the force of the cold wind whipping against his face. Never had the park held quite the meaning it did that morning. Hearing the echoing of galloping hooves, Sarah, also an early bird, threw open her window and leant out to see what was going on.

'John! What brings you here?'

'Hoist the flag!' John yelled back as he clattered up to the front door, waving his stick towards the tower. 'We have a son! A son for Ravensworth!'

Blind though he might be, Sir Giles was not deaf. John's excited voice rang out loud and clear through the still, crisp air, reaching his father as he lay in his room overlooking the park, above the drawing-room.

'What's that?' Sir Giles heaved himself up and tugged at the bell-pull, which he could find by instinct. 'What are they saying?'

Hardly had the deep peal sounded through the house than the bedroom door flew open. On the threshold stood John, booted and spurred, his face glowing from his gallop.

'Sir, you have your grandson! A Red Ravensworth!' Grinning, John bowed deeply towards the bed. 'He is one John Duncan.'

'Hey! So you've got a child at last; good. A son too.' The old man, the tassel wagging in approval on his bed-cap, beamed in pleasure at his youngest son. 'Give my love and congratulations to that wife of yours and tell her I'll be down later on to see him for myself. I'm not so blind that I can't see my own grandson!' He gave a chuckle.

They were still talking when, down in the village, the church bells began to peal, proclaiming to all the world the glad tidings of a son, across the snow clad Cotswolds. It was many years since the bells had rung out for a Ravensworth son. They reached Emily at the other end of the village and she smiled. The world was a wonderful place.

John Duncan was christened in Ravensworth Church, one Sunday in March. Throughout the ceremony, he had lain quietly in his godmother's arms, only whimpering like a puppy at rare intervals. Sarah had taken her duties very seriously, as she renounced the Devil and all his works. She wondered how she would be able to fulfil her duties, for no doubt he would be no angel as he grew up. Once her godson had been tempted to try the acoustics of the old church, with devastating results, and he refrained from a repeat performance. It was a happy christening and the whole family gathered for the occasion, to gladden Sir Giles' heart. Since Duncan's arrival the old man had taken on a new lease of life, and had not been so well for a long time.

As Duncan grew, he spent more and more time with his grandfather, and they were often to be seen on fine days driving together in the park. Sometimes Emily would accompany them, but more often than not, he went alone, the old man enjoying his grandson's company. Duncan came to look for these outings and would wait for the familiar crunch of his grandfather's carriage on the gravel.

John, stiil serving in the Army, had recently been promoted to a Lieutenant-Colonel, and his duties required much time in Town. They liked their town house, overlooking the Park, but after a while Emily found it better, except on rare occasions, to leave Duncan and his nanny in Sarah's care at the Towers, where she now reigned in Aunt Julia's stead. For Sarah, these visits were a mixed blessing. She loved the small boy and looked forward to his arrival, but his flaming red head marked an equally hot temper. If crossed, he would fly into a raging temper and stamp and scream. On the first occasion he tried this, Sarah was picking off dead blooms in the rose garden.

'Won't – won't!' Duncan's shrill voice grew louder and louder.

'And what won't you do, young sir?' Sir Giles rounded the corner of the stable-yard, guiding his steps with a stick in one hand and his eldest son's arm in the other.

'Oh, Grandpa. I want to ride Tempest. Say I can. Please. Please, Grandpa.' The small red face, blotched with tears of rage, looked up with pleading into the old wrinkled face above him. Needless to say, Grandpa knew how to deal with young terrors and refused to give way, though secretly he was delighted with his grandson's show of courage, for Tempest, John's new hunter, was no easy ride and had earned his name. He was only at the Towers because no groom at the Dower House could ride him and John did not want him in London.

Unfortunately, this became a usual occurrence. Escaping from his nanny, Duncan would make his way down from his nursery and out to the stables, where he would enjoy himself by the hour until found and retrieved. Once he even managed to take his sturdy little person down to the kennels, only to be brought back an hour later by Tom the huntsman, kicking and protesting at the top of his lungs. No amount of protest had availed, and he was marched off to bed, scarlet in the face and yelling hard. A week later, his nanny left. She had been supplanted by the still capable, though ageing, Miss Dinmore. With her aid, Sarah was able to control his more wild flights of fancy and peace was restored to the Towers.

The days of Edward VII's reign had run out all too soon. And as the day of the coronation of their new king, King George V, and Queen Mary, drew near, Emily started to lay her plans for the entertainment of her family, for their London home lent itself superbly to the occasion. Anne and Harriet had already expressed their wish to bring their families up for the big day to watch the procession; and Sarah and Charles had prevailed upon their father to join the party and come to London to be with them.

The eve of the big day dawned and the town house became crammed to the ceilings. Every available bed was full. The children, including Duncan, now under the guidance of Miss Dinmore, were crowded into the nurseries, and were eagerly awaiting the big moment. They were fortunate. Emily's front windows overlooked part of the Royal route, giving them a perfect view.

'Aunt Emily. Where's Uncle John?' Elizabeth, Harriet's youngest, peered anxiously through the panes. Somewhere in the colourful procession rode John, in full dress.

Duncan, firmly held by his Uncle Charles, gave an excited squawk.

'Papa! Papa!' Away down below, riding erect and gravely at the head of his contingent, came the familiar figure of his father. Slowly he trotted past on Black Knight. The old hunter had proved his worth and in his old age was enjoying his life in London, for with age had at last come discretion, and the old horse had been a good choice, though at first he had been rather lively. Next week he would return to Ravensworth with the family.

Chapter XI

The ugly rumblings of war had flared up into the true thing three years before, and shortly after its outbreak, Charles, prevented by his leg from serving his Country, had converted the Towers into a convalescent home for officers coming back from the horrors of the Great War that raged across the Channel. In this he had been backed by his sister, for they were now alone at the Towers. Sir Giles, tired and old, had been unable to withstand the grave shock and had died within the first winter, a sad and shaken man, leaving his eldest son to carry on the family in his stead. Soon, as the numbers increased, Charles and Sarah found it necessary to move out of the Towers altogether and join forces with Emily and Duncan at the Dower House, from where they could all take a very active part in their chosen war work.

Hardly had the news of the outbreak reached Ravensworth than John had been posted with his regiment to the front. Daily, Emily scanned the papers and waited for news of her husband. At first news had reached regularly, but in recent weeks she had heard nothing. Somewhere, right in the thick of it, was John – whether alive or dead she knew not. Since the spring, men from his regiment had been arriving daily from the front, for the benefit of the peace and quiet of the hills that played such a large part in their recuperation, but none of them could give her any news. Worry and little sleep began to tell on her that long summer. Every day, she hoped fervently that someone would have met John somewhere and could give her the news she sought. October and her wedding anniversary – their eighteenth – came and went, and so did November and most of December, and still no news. Christmas was upon them, and Duncan, now a sturdy ten-year-old, resembling his Uncle Charles, save for his colouring, was once more home from his prep school for the holidays.

'Mama – Mama – where are you?' Duncan came hurrying into the house, having run all the way from the Towers. He often went up to talk to the lads and enjoyed hearing about the war. 'You know that nice lad, the young one with the red hair like mine, that came in yesterday on crutches? Well . . .'

'Yes, dear.' Emily, a cold shiver running down her spine, looked enquiringly at her son. His face told her all she needed to know.

The clouds of war lifted slowly, but for Emily, the world had gone blank. Her whole life had been John's life and now he would never come home again. With a mixture of sorrow and gratitude, she looked back over their many happy years together. For they had been happy and so contented. Now it was hard to realize she would never see or hear him again, though it would be many years before his familiar voice and footsteps ceased to ring in her ears and make her turn to look for the beloved face that accompanied them. A strong willed woman, she went about her many activities as usual, and save for her sombre black, few would have known what she had gone through. Sarah, watching her sister-in-law's efforts, felt distressed. She could see below the façade that hid the real Emily from the world, and was helpless to shield her from its harshness. Only time could make amends.

Everywhere around them, their friends went gay. The large parties of pre-war days were once more in full swing and the Ravensworths found themselves swept ruthlessly into their whirl. The motor car was no longer a thing of surprise; everyone had one. Slowly it was deposing the horse. Even up at the Towers, a small corner of the coach house had been given over to a high wheeled affair that Charles drove in state round the countryside.

The New Year following the end of the war saw many changes, one of which was the return of the family to the Towers, during that spring. With the last of the convalescents gone, Charles had been anxious to move back into his own home and take up the reins of office in earnest.

'Emily, my dear, what are you going to do?' asked Charles, one evening after dinner, shortly before their move. The thick curtains had been drawn across the windows, and the three of them sat quietly before the fire talking – they did a lot of talking these days, for Charles, like Sarah, was worried about Emily. She had made no mention of her own plans and he hated the thought of leaving her alone at the Dower House. The town house had been sold at the beginning of the war, when she had moved to the country for good.

'I don't know; what can I do? I've Duncan to think of. He's my main concern, he needs a true home to come to in the holidays. Otherwise as you know, except for the servants, I'm alone for a good nine months of every year.'

'Quite so; that is what Sarah and I feel. We wish you and Duncan would come to us, and make your real home at the Towers. It is not good for you here, or at least won't be once we have gone, and there is room and to spare at home, and you know it. So do say you will come.' Charles voice held conviction. It was sincere, not just an empty invitation given out of pity. Emily wanted no pity and no one knew that better than Charles and Sarah.

Silence fell on the room. The firelight flickered and made patterns over the carpet. Lazing on the hearthrug, toasting its tummy in the blazing heat, stretched a black labrador. Emily had not the heart to banish Burn, for she had been John's.

'That's welcome too, and can have the run of the house!' Charles had read Emily's thoughts. 'And the rest of your animals, everything can come.'

'Thanks, all right, I'll come.'

Emily blew her sharp nose and kept her eyes lowered to the carpet. She did not like to trust herself to look up for a moment or two. She was more grateful than she would have cared to own. Now the decision had been made, Emily was thankful. She hated the thought of leaving the Dower House, her home for nearly thirty years, but it held too many memories for the present; she must break away and start afresh.

Charles had little trouble in finding a tenant for the Dower House. Now, with the decrease in servants, there was a ready demand for the smaller type of country house, and the Dower House could be run on a small staff.

Duncan, hearing of the proposed move in a letter from his mother, was delighted. The Dower House was small, and the Towers had for so long been his home that he looked on it as almost his own. The estate, too, offered greater scope for a growing schoolboy, and he looked forward to his holidays in familiar surroundings. John, fearing he might not return this time, had left his small son to his brother's guardianship, and before long Duncan came to look on his uncle more as a father than an uncle, which was hardly surprising, his own father having been absent for the last three years of his life. Slowly, during those last four years, Duncan had turned more and more to his uncle for help and guidance. John, in his wisdom, had realized his small son needed a man to control him, and without his father might well have become too much for his mother single handed. As it was, Duncan's temper had been brought under control and the lad had learnt that he could not always get his own way by ranting and raging. Under his uncle's watchful eye, the small boy soon started to follow in his footsteps and to fish and shoot. As he progressed, Charles let him join the guns on the smaller shoots and many happy hours would be spent tramping the homelands, the lame man and the small, red headed lad walking side by side. The farm, too, held its attractions and Charles enjoyed nothing more than to take his small nephew down with him on his rounds of the estate. As he grew, Duncan spent more time helping in the fields during the long summer holidays and often he was joined by a few of his school friends who came to stay. He was an intelligent lad and the farm workers soon found they could trust him; for, provided he was kept really busy, he was happy.

Besides fishing and shooting, Duncan also rode. Sir Giles, after the first tempestuous scene, had, after a suitable time had elapsed, given him a tiny fat Icelandic pony of his very own. It was his pride and joy, and soon the pair of them were to be seen all over the park. Then there had been bigger ponies and now his last one was sadly outgrown after several years of partnership and would soon be going to one of his cousins.

Coming home for their first Christmas at the Towers, Duncan found a new face sticking out of his box. As he walked down the long row of boxes, a white face shot out over the partition, nearly knocking him over.

'Hi, hallo, who are you?' Duncan stroked the soft neck that had stretched down to greet him.

'Evening, Master Duncan. That's Rattler. He's yours.'

Paddy touched his forelock as he spoke and then stepped forward to open the door, catching hold of the headcollar as he did so. 'Whoa, boy. Come then. Come on my boy.' Crooning to the horse, he stripped off the rugs to reveal a glossy chestnut coat.

'Oh, he's a stunner! How big is he?' Duncan reached up with his hand to the withers, and gently laid it on. 'He's huge!' In ecstasy, he ran his hand along the strong back, feeling the muscles ripple as it went.

'He's just over fifteen hands and six years old. Like him, my boy?' Uncle Charles had come in unheard and had been standing in the doorway watching his nephew, and quickly cut short Duncan's stammered thanks. 'That's all right; he's your Christmas present. Foam was too small to hunt this winter. So I've given Rattler to you now. By the way, hounds meet at Aunt Anne's tomorrow, so it will be an early start.'

How Duncan loved his home! He was never dull; there was always something for him to do. His mother, once away from the Dower House and its memories, had quickly regained her old happiness. This season, she too was hunting again and had rather a nice dark brown mare, the last daughter of her old grey. The Towers held so many happy memories that Emily soon found that they overshadowed the less happy ones and by degrees she could talk and think of John without pain.

The days drifted into months; and on into years. The seasons came and went, and many visits were exchanged between the Towers and Anne's and Harriet's families. To Emily, these were contented days; especially her long summer visits to Harriet. Unlike Sarah, who had grown into an extremely practical woman with a downright manner and more commonsense than feelings, Harriet was kind and gentle, and of all the sisters, held a very special place in Emily's heart, and in the first few years that followed John's death, the younger Emily found herself turning more and more to Harriet in thankfulness.

One of the biggest changes at the Towers since the war was the innovation of a tennis court. On the hilly, undulating ground, it had set quite a problem. No one could agree as to where it was to go. In the end, after much argument and a certain amount of heartburning, it was relegated to the nearest walled garden, a corner of which was sacrificed, much to the regret of Moss the gardener. It made an excellent situation, and many gay and noisy parties took place there. With the increasing popularity of the car, a wider locality was opened up and friends drawn from a greater and wider field. The ten miles that separated Anne's brood and their children from their uncle's place become nothing, and they were constant visitors, along with Harriet's, who came to stay on the slightest pretext and were frequently to be found at the Towers. In the holidays, the big house was seldom empty for more than a few days at a time, and rang with merry laughter.

'Mother, you know last holidays, you asked me if I had made up my mind yet – what I want to do when I leave school next summer.' Duncan was standing with his back to the fireplace, a hand in either pocket, his dark eyes staring out under bushy red eyebrows. He was a typical youth of his day and age, with his share of good looks and a pleasant nature.

'Yes. I remember. Decided?' Emily had dreaded this moment, not that she was selfish, far from it, but he was her all, and she dreaded losing him. It would be years yet before he married, and she wanted him to go to Oxford. Charles had voiced no opinion either way – as far as she knew, he was playing 'possum'.

'Mother. I want to go to Sandhurst, please.' Dropping his steady gaze from her face, he continued quickly, 'Don't say no. I fully realize that you would rather I didn't, but I must. Dad would have wanted it, I know he would. Just before he left, he told me he hoped one day I would also follow in his footsteps. So you see, I want to, more than anything on earth. There is no other life for me. Uncle Charles does know. I told him tonight before dinner. He agrees, if you will. It's a good life, Guy enjoys it, I have talked to him about it, and to Harry, though I don't think I would care for the Navy. I prefer a life that will give me time to enjoy the country as well.' He gave a little chuckle. His mother's face was a study. The inevitable had happened. There was nothing Emily could do, so she held her peace. Duncan waited to see if his mother would express any views, then he continued, his voice having taken on a serious note in place of the rather defiant one he had used at first.

'I know what you are afraid of, Mother, but the Army in peacetime is a good life and there won't be another war. That was the war to end all wars. Anyway, I'm not Uncle Charles' heir, so there's no drawback on that score. I know that Grandpa used to treat me as such, but I am quite aware that Uncle James lies next in line for Ravensworth and most likely has a horde of sons and daughters. Hang it all, look how many Aunt Anne and Aunt Harriet have. There are sixteen there alone, with Aunt Anne's seven to Aunt Harriet's nine; so heaven only knows how many Uncle James may have by now. Because we've never heard from them doesn't mean that one day they won't breeze in out of the blue and claim their inheritance when the time comes. So why let us worry on that score? Anyway, it's a morbid thought and I am the last person to sit at home and wait for something that is not even mine.'

Emily had to be content with this, for she knew only too well that what Duncan said was true. It was just that she had lost John, and was loath to see Duncan follow in his footsteps, though really she knew she should be proud and grateful that he had decided to serve his King and Country. As for the inheritance, well, the Ravensworths did have large families and always had had. The fact that she and John had had only one child was beside the point. Somewhere in the New World, James had settled; but beyond that first letter that she had seen, no one had heard of another. If one had arrived, Sir Giles had never mentioned it.

Chapter XII

Duncan loved the Army, and never regretted his decision of six years before. It was a grand life, for besides the more serious soldiering, which he enjoyed, he still had ample time to see his home during his leave and the opportunity to fish and shoot, not to mention hunting. With a wide circle of friends, he seldom lacked companions to share his many interests. Stationed on the outskirts of London, the bright lights were readily available to him. Soon his presence was looked for by the match-making mamas, who under the false impression that he was his uncle's heir to the rolling acres of the Cotswolds around his native Ravensworth, hunted him unmercifully. They were out for a good catch and this made him chuckle, as they were to be disappointed. For Duncan danced with them all, in his gay and happy manner – and passed on!

Caroline Brandon looked across the paddock at the local point-to-point. The stiff wind whipped her long black hair into a tangle round her face. Petulantly, she tossed it out of her way. Unlike other girls of her generation, she continued to wear her hair to her thin sloping shoulders, where it turned under in a bob, framing her long, horse-shaped features. Groomed to the last hair, she stood out amongst the tweed clad spectators that lined the ropes, several deep, eager to see their particular fancy parade before the members' race. Down in the corner, the lashing hooves of a powerful chestnut caught her eye. What was this? It was worth investigating.

Caroline was a stranger to the Cotswolds. The anxious faces, waiting for the mounting bell, were unknown to her. Visiting friends in the neighbourhood, she was finding herself extremely bored. The country air made her feel sleepy, and as far as she could see, there was nothing to be gained from living there. The people were dull and the entertainment, nil. London, in her opinion, was the only civilized place to live. It was alive, there was always something to do, parties to attend, young men to take her out and make a fuss of her. She was beginning to wish she had refused the Washfords' invitation. There they were, talking away happily to their friends, a bunch of cabbages.

Yorkshire born, she had left her home in a small North-Country town, nestling between the moors and the sea, at the first opportunity, dragging her wretched parents with her for the Season. She was fortunate; they worshipped their only daughter and were loaded with this world's goods and would do anything for her, returning season after season to satisfy her whims. Now, at nearly twenty-three, she was hard and callous, out entirely for herself. People who knew her shied off as from a tiger before they too got caught in her deadly claws.

Working her way round the crowds, she came level with the restless chestnut. Close too, he was magnificent. Standing well over sixteen hands and closely knit, he presented a powerful picture of charged dynamite. To a more knowledgeable spectator, his pawing of the ground and rolling of the whites of his eyes would have given fair warning, but on Caroline they were wasted. She had no eyes for the horse, only the red headed man, standing a little way off, talking to an older woman, slightly apart from the rest of their group. Casting a fleeting glance in their direction, Caroline deemed that they must be related, when the man with a limp moved across to join them.

'Ready Duncan?' Uncle Charles turned to his nephew as the mounting bell rang.

'Yes, thank you, sir. I'll hold him for the first circuit, then let him go through.'

He sounded confident. His voice, drifting over to the girl on the rails, had an odd lilt to it. It was nice. Swiftly thumbing through her card she read: No. 13. 'Red Devil' – Chestnut gelding – 7 years – by Red Rival out of Devil-May-Care. Owner-rider: Captain Duncan Ravensworth (Ravensworth Foxhounds).

'Hum. So that was it. Well, Caroline my girl, maybe this won't be such a dull week-end after all. We'll see.' The girl pocketed her card and moved off towards the course.

Red Devil, quoted at 20-1, had never run before and was an unknown quantity. To Duncan, astride his back, he felt like a volcano. With every yard to the post, he seemed to erupt.

'Steady, steady boy, steady now!' Gently he stroked the dripping neck, arched in front of him. His heart had long since descended to his boots and he felt sick and empty. Was he a fool? Surely Red Devil would never start. Worse and worse thoughts raced through his mind, each one more terrifying than the last.

The paddock was situated on the side of a hill, overlooking the course which ran round the far hillside and back through the valley. The long journey from the paddock to the course seemed never ending, as Duncan carefully wove his way through the throngs of people that crowded round the bookmakers, strung out in a long line along the crest of the hill. Overhead the April sun shone down from a cloudless sky, turning the newly breaking trees a glistening green tinged with yellow, while underfoot, the new grass made a brave effort to show its head, only to be trampled down again by a thousand feet till it turned brown and withered. Everywhere, the atmosphere was charged with excitement and anticipation. Some of it must have communicated itself to the Red Devil, for without warning he reared up and struck out with a foreleg, his sharp ears laid flat back along his lean neck and his wild eyes rolling. In all directions, the crowds fled out of the big horse's path. Everyone, that is, save for the black haired girl. Caroline was lost in thought and cared not where she went. With perfect nonchalance and to the horror of the spectators who looked on helplessly, she wandered right into the path of the maddened horse. Oblivious of the danger in which she stood, Caroline looked up puzzled as the crowds started to shout. The more the noise, the greater the fury on the part of the horse; the chestnut was being driven mad. Duncan, helpless on the vertical back, struggled valiantly to stick on. Should he try and pull him over backwards – and crash on the great crowd that had gathered behind him – or try and force him down? Looking down, he became aware of the flowing black hair framing two startled blue eyes. Unblinkingly, they gazed spellbound into his scarlet face. Desperately, he tried to guide the wavering horse to one side. It was impossible for a living soul to reach his head and lead him to safety.

The sickening scream that rent the air echoed round the hills and went through Duncan like a knife. The Red Devil was down at last; so was the girl. All around them the crowds closed in.

Leaving the paddock as soon as her son mounted, Emily and the rest of the Ravensworth party were unaware of the commotion. For Sir Charles it was his big day. The reputation of his hounds depended on it for their good will. Taking up their positions on the waggon overlooking the finish, the paddock was out of sight and the noise was drowned in the roar from the bookmakers calling the last minute odds.

'Look here, sir, I'm sorry about this. Can I do anything?' Duncan had dismounted and was talking to one of the officials.

'No, go on down. There's nothing you can do, even if you do stay. You must go down and race. You can't withdraw now.' The official had known Duncan all his life and felt sorry for him. He had been powerless to prevent it.

'But, sir—'

'No, Duncan, go on down.'

Reluctantly, Duncan remounted and cantered down to the start, his face as white as chalk. The ribald remarks from his fellow riders failed to bring any quick repartee. Instead, all the while, before him danced the image of the girl with flowing black hair and huge blue eyes, that had looked so steadily up at him as he fought with his mount. Her ear-piercing scream as he knocked her down haunted him. He had waited for the stretcher party to arrive and bear her off to the safety of the first-aid tent, before riding half-heartedly to the post. Hardly had he arrived than the flag went up. They were under starter's orders. In another second, they would be off. All of a sudden his temper got the better of him. Duncan screwed up his face. Why, what right had a silly girl, dressed fit for Bond Street, to wander into his path, little fool. Gritting his teeth, he gathered himself together, collected all the power of his great chestnut under him and waited. All orders from his uncle gone to the wind. Duncan, now, was in a flaming temper. His face was set in a grim mask and hands held Red Devil in a grip of iron as he waited impatiently for the flag to drop. Inside him his temper was reaching boiling-point and in another second would come right over!

'They're off!'

The loud roar went up from the crowd and acted as a whip to the fretting chestnut, who was trembling in every taut muscle. He shot forward as from a gun and swiftly took up the running, driven on by his reckless rider. The first fence came and went: Duncan hardly even felt the big horse rise for it, and within a second, they were galloping on to the next. This, too, came and went like the first, and so on down the long course, till the big, wide water loomed up broad and fearsome in their path. The big chestnut had a thing about water and Duncan knew it. Relentlessly he drove him on. Swish! They had hit the top of the fence as he flattened out. Splash! They had landed half in, half out of the water, but with a stumble they regained the bank and galloped on. The next few fences gave as little trouble as the first. Down the long hill they raced to the fence at the bottom and then up the stiff pull to the finishing post for the first time.

Sir Charles, thunderstruck, watched his nephew's progress over the first circuit, through his glasses.

'What on earth is the young fool up to?' The glasses fell from a nerveless grasp as the chestnut swept past the post and started on the second circuit. 'He'll cook that horse if he rides like that. How many times have I to tell him!'

Emily and Sarah remained silent. Something had gone wrong, they were sure, for they could sense it in the air. Emily had known her son too long to believe that even he would let his temper go that extent, or at least she hoped so!

Reaching the end of the roped part of the course where the horses came and went from the paddock, the Red Devil swung right, stopped dead in his tracks, and reared. Up, up he went, striking at the air with his forelegs, while behind them thundered the rest of the field, who within seconds had swept past and vanished into the distance. Would the great horse ever come down? Duncan began to wonder. Coming into the straight, he had had a good lead over his nearest rival and though the pace had begun to tell on his own horse, he still had some reserve. Now all that was wasted. With the last horse disappearing into the valley, Red Devil dropped to the ground again and stood surveying the expectant crowds. Then, shaking his head, he set off in pursuit of the others.

Would he ever make up the tremendous leeway? Duncan, now at last in control of his mount, with his own temper cooled off, set about the almost impossible task that lay ahead.

Emily, who had given a gasp as the horse had stopped and reared, dropped her hands from her eyes.

'He can't. But wait, he's going to!'

Duncan's whole mind was now on the job and yard by yard he relentlessly closed the gap between himself and the rear horses that lay between him and victory. Through unblinking eyes, blinded by the rushing wind beating against his face, Duncan rode resolutely on. This was a challenge like no other challenge he had yet received. He had a good horse and he knew it, but could he ride it? Now was his chance. For the first time since their partnership had begun eighteen months before, Duncan felt himself on terms with his horse. The link had at last been forged that would hold them together, and help them to understand one another, through the rough and the smooth. They were at last partners, and Duncan was beginning to enjoy his ride after all. By the time they had cleared the last but one fence down in the bottom of the valley, Red Devil had caught and passed the rear of the field. Stride by stride, Duncan pushed him on. With a panther-like spring, the big horse sailed over the last fence and set off on the hardest part of all. From the crowds, the great roar went up, chanting out the name of the favourite.

'Whippoorwill! Whippoorwill!'

The mighty roar died as it had risen. From the rear came the gallant chestnut Red Devil, straining every muscle within his powerful body.

On their hay-wain, Emily, supported on either side by Sarah and Charles, with Anne and Harriet and their families grouped behind her, watched spell-bound and then took up the roar with the crowds, and was shouting with the best of them. Inch by inch, Red Devil gained on Whippoorwill. His tail, his rump, his girth, his shoulder, then his long lean neck, stretched out as far as it would go, fighting off the challenge; then at last his head. Gallantly, the little bay strove to hold off the big chestnut. The post came nearer and nearer; then with ears pricked, Red Devil swept past.

Duncan relaxed, dropped his hands on the Devil's shoulders, and slumped exhausted in his saddle for a brief second.

'Good boy; you've made it.' Gently he stroked he soaking neck and shoulder.

As if in reply, Red Devil rose once more and waved his hooves to the stunned and admiring crowds, in acknowledgement!

Back in the unsaddling enclosure, Duncan's first thoughts were for the black haired girl.

'Don't worry, she's all right sir. A passing blow on the shoulder, and shock. She may have broken her collar bone, that's all. Nothing serious.' The steward spoke reassuringly.

'Thank heavens, for that! Who is she anyway? Do you know?'

Duncan cast a glance over his shoulder in time to see his family threading their way through the surging crowd. It had certainly been a race. Out in the crowds, many disgruntled punters cursed openly, and those who on principle always hung onto their tickets to the bitter end, rejoiced at their good fortune, as they wended their way to collect their winnings from the disgusted bookmakers. A twenty-to-one winner under those circumstances luckily was not often found and they shrugged their shoulders as they handed over large wads of notes, for Duncan had been backed by many who were loyal to the Ravensworths.

Many hours later, in the Cotswold stone cottage hospital that lay on a bleak hillside overlooking the neighbouring town, Caroline Brandon woke to find herself in a small white walled room that smelt of clean disinfectant and well scrubbed floors. Puzzled, she tried to collect her wits. Where was she? How did she get there? It certainly was not her room at the Washfords'. Then, a sharp pain in her shoulder as she tried to turn over reminded her of the nightmare that had assailed her at the races.

'Oh, yes, that brute of a horse and its red headed rider.'

Caroline shut her eyes again and continued her thoughts.

'I smiled engagingly at a glorious vision in an emerald pullover with chocolate cross hoops and an emerald and chocolate quartered cap, who crossed my path – and then wham! I was down. Not a nice way to treat a girl who had smiled so sweetly up at him.' She felt aggrieved. He would find it harder to throw Caroline Brandon over than that. Before, she might have just been whiling away her idle week-end; now she was in earnest. Her interest was no longer a passing fancy – it was the real thing. There was money there; that was obvious. His relations, if those had been they, were, even if they looked a trifle stuffy and tweedy, well off. Those tweed suits on the women had been tailor made and expensive. No doubt about that. Caroline knew good clothes when she saw them. That brute of a horse, too, he had not been bought for nothing. No doubt that lame man had been responsible for that.

At the back of her mind, something was troubling Caroline. The name Ravensworth kept turning over and over and just failing to slip into its right niche. Caroline's mind was a series of niches in which she stored her social news. Drifting between waking and sleeping, her mind continued its endless circle. Somewhere, somehow, she knew that name. Then just as she was nearly asleep, it dawned on her.

'Why, of course, what a fool I've been!' Caroline said to herself with a dry chuckle, which would have made Emily's heart turn over if she could have heard it and seen the expression on the girl's face. 'The Red Ravensworth. The uncatchable. Well, we'll see!'

With that Caroline fell asleep.

Chapter XIII

Emily, learning after the race of the odd encounter between her own Duncan and the black haired Caroline, had a strange foreboding. If ever there was a calculating minx, then here was one in this girl. For Emily was no fool and knew of Caroline's reputation already, and could see nothing but frustration and sadness coming out of a liaison between the two.

In spite of his mother's warning not to get mixed up with Caroline Brandon, Duncan set off the following morning, armed with a large bunch of flowers, to visit her in hospital. A magnet drew him there against his better judgement. Ever since Red Devil's memorable race, he had been unable to forget her face as he had looked down from his great height – a face that had imprinted itself on his mind. Parking his sports car in the forecourt of the hospital, Duncan entered the great doors and looked around.

'Can I help you, sir?' A voice from the reception desk made him look up. Quickly, he made his request. 'Why, certainly you may see her now, Captain Ravensworth. How nice of you to call. Come this way please, Nurse will show you to her room.' Duncan found himself handed over to a young nurse, who led him down a series of passages to a door at the end of the wing, overlooking the gardens. 'Miss Brandon is in here.'

Lying there in a white fluffy bedjacket, with her long black hair falling in cascades over her sparkling white pillows while her arm rested interestingly in a spotless white sling across her chest, Caroline looked enchanting. From her bed, her blue eyes looked up in wonderment, as Duncan, quietly following in the wake of the nurse, entered her room. It was as if she was seeing another vision. Inside, she had a feeling of triumph. And to herself she thought,

'Caroline, my girl, this is going to be easy. Play your cards right and you have him on your hook. But steady does it.'

With these none too commendable thoughts uppermost in her mind, she returned his gaze with her sweetest and most alluring smile. The wary would have been warned, but Duncan was blind to all warnings at that moment. All caution was thrown to the wind. He was captivated and enchanted by the black haired girl. She was different, she was exciting. Why had he not met her before? Caroline turned on all the charm she possessed, and the hour fled without either of them noticing it. The sound of soft footsteps sounded outside the door and then the young nurse looked in to say Miss Brandon must now rest. With great reluctance, Duncan rose to leave.

'Captain Ravensworth, you will come and see me again, won't you?' Caroline used her silkiest voice, and Duncan, looking down at her lying there, was not proof against those long black lashes that blinked so piteously, and the blue eyes that gazed so beseechingly up at him.

'Of course, I will. I will be along tomorrow, never fear.'

With a wave of his hand he walked out of her room, but unfortunately not out of her life. True to his word, despite his mother's entreaties to the contrary, Duncan turned up the following afternoon at Caroline's bedside with another peace offering of fruit and flowers. Throughout that week, Duncan's sports car became a familiar sight speeding along the country roads between Ravensworth and the hospital. All the town knew of his odd encounter with the girl and the subsequent visits to her in hospital. By the end of the week, gossip was rife. Everyone was linking their names.

'But Mother, it's the least we can do.' Duncan was sitting in the garden with his mother, towards the end of the week following the point-to-point.

'I realize that, Duncan. But she has other friends. After all she was the Washfords' guest. Can't she go back there for a while?'

Emily was, she knew, fighting a losing battle, but fight it she would while she had any breath left in her body, for she valued her son and refused to stand by and see his whole life ruined.

'Come, Mother, we must have her. It's the least we can do, after what happened. So please say yes, just for me.' Duncan, too, had charm and was using it at this moment to further his own ends. Caroline had completely ensnared him in her wicked coil. Not for nothing had she earned her reputation, but this time she really wanted her victim for her very own, not just a passing plaything.

Emily, in the end, much against her better judgement, gave in. Naturally, what Duncan had said was true. If the girl really had nowhere to go, and the Washfords were making no effort to have her back, then as a Christian, it was her duty to ask the girl to convalesce at the Towers.

Caroline once more was getting her way. Playing her cards carefully, she engineered a long visit – right through to the bitter end of Duncan's leave. From the very first moment of setting eyes on her going down to the post, Duncan had been as a rabbit with a stoat.

The summer that followed was one of constant strife between mother and son, as the whirlwind courtship came to a climax soon after their return to London. The engagement was short and they were married in London towards the end of June. It was a big fashionable wedding. The world was there. Caroline's parents were rich and loved nothing better than to make a show and splash their wealth round. Nothing was too good or too expensive for their daughter. In Emily, every nerve and feeling felt revolted. She was nearly heart-broken; her own plans for her son had been so very different. She longed for a daughter-in-law whom she could love; instead she had gained one whom she could only detest and despise, though in all fairness, she did try very hard to like the girl once she realized she was powerless to prevent the marriage. From the first, it had been inevitable, but until it had become a *fait accompli*, she had refused to give up hope of over-throwing the girl's schemes. She might have succeeded, but for one thing: she could not reckon with her son, now independent and able to snap his fingers in his family's face. So amid much rejoicing and celebration on the part of the Brandon family – the uncatchable was caught!

Despite her feelings, Emily had put on a good face for the wedding, but her worst fears were soon realized. From then on, their only news was gleaned from the society papers. The Towers neither saw nor heard from Duncan and his wife. Evidently, Caroline was living a life fast and furious. Nevertheless, when, the following winter, shortly before Christmas, an announcement appeared in the papers, she tried to forgive them wholeheartedly.

'Sarah, have you seen this?' Emily held out a copy of *The Times*, her face wreathed in smiles.

'No, what is it? It sounds exciting.' They had formed a habit of late of reading the morning papers over their mid-morning coffee, to exchange bits of gossip and news.

'Here, read it for yourself.' Emily pointed to the birth column.

'RAVENSWORTH. In Yorkshire, to Caroline (née Brandon) wife of Captain John Duncan Ravensworth of . . . Regiment. a daughter.'

'Congratulations, Emily, on your first grandchild.' Sarah beamed with pleasure across at her sister-in-law and life long friend. 'May it be the first of many!'

The pleasure and happiness that the announcement brought was, however, short lived. Overjoyed, Emily wrote straight away to express her delight at the news. For days she waited – for weeks – for months – still no letter came. The dreadful silence that had reigned since the wedding continued unabated. Duncan might not be alive, he was so utterly and completely cut off from his own home and family. It was Charles, some six months later, on one of his rare visits to London, who, bumping into a mutual friend at his club, learnt, quite by chance, that the baby had been christened Anne, after her great-aunt. Beyond this, Charles was unable to glean much, either of Duncan and his family or of its present whereabouts. It was certainly an unhappy state of affairs and the Ravensworths could only hope that in time, Duncan would return to his home and the breach between the two generations would be healed. That Caroline was behind the breach, no one doubted; Duncan was as putty in her hands. She called the piper and he danced to her tune. In many ways, Duncan was not unlike his Uncle James; they were both throwbacks to some ancestor who had left his character indelibly stamped for evermore on his successors. Duncan, too, was that rare thing, a red Ravensworth. There had only been about three in the long history of the Ravensworths – each one had been noted for his temper!

Life at the Towers continued in much the same way as it had done for the last half century; once more the old place was quiet and orderly, for no longer was the place invaded by hordes of happy, laughing young people who had come for the gay and impromptu dances and wild tennis parties that Duncan had delighted in. Charles still hunted his own hounds once a week, while on the other days, the first whip carried the horn in his place. Charles was beginning to find his lame leg a slight handicap and could no longer get about as he used to do. As for Sarah and Emily, they still rode regularly to hounds throughout the season, and found time for the many committee meetings and other good works in which they were expected to play a leading part, as a matter of course. Their lives were full and useful.

With the death of King George, Charles began to feel old; after all, they had been born in the same year. It is always sad to see one's own contemporaries go, for the truth is brought home to one so much more forcibly. There is no escaping from it. Sarah and Emily, years younger than Charles, could not share his feelings in quite the same way. For them, life was still young and they had many years ahead of them yet. So when the first stunning shock of the news had passed away, they settled back into their everyday routine and continued much as before, only digging themselves out of the Cotswolds and Ravensworth the following year for the coronation of their new King and Queen in Westminster Abbey at the beginning of May.

While they were in London for the occasion, Charles looked up from his morning paper and said with a twinkle:

'Here, Emily, this will interest you.'

'What, Charles?' Emily waited expectantly, her head tilted slightly to one side. In middle age, she was a remarkably good looking woman – with age had come a quiet charm like her mother's.

'This – you've got a grandson this time and its been born in Yorkshire like the first. Congratulations, my dear.' Charles handed over the paper so that Emily could see for herself. It made her day and she was beside herself with delight. Once again she was to know disappointment at its bitterest. Would she never see Duncan again?

As the months turned into years, she began to wonder.

The long separation was beginning to tell on Emily's health. Night after night, she would lie awake in her room at the Towers – just thinking. This state of affairs went on till the long expected and dreaded news broke over the world on that September morning in 1939.

The family had just emerged from church and were standing in the sun talking to their friends. At the gate stood their trap. Charles still liked to drive to the old church in the village, as he had done all his life, behind a horse. This Sunday had been no exception. The news was so shattering – it was as if the world had stood still.

Two days later the unexpected happened. Up the long drive, a low slung roadster made its way. Entering by way of the southern gate to the park, Duncan steered his car carefully along past the lake and over the well remembered hump-backed bridge that spanned the River Raven, and so on till at last the great gate-tower came in sight, dark against the night sky. Seeing his old home he loved so dearly, standing there in the moonlight, a lump came to his throat. How could he have been so blind, and withheld the impulse to return for so long. It had, of course, been Caroline who had been instrumental in the complete break between mother and son. She hated and, worst still, feared her mother-in-law, for she knew Emily had a great pull over her son, and she had no intention of sharing him with anyone – least of all his mother and family. Tonight, she was in ignorance of his whereabouts; knowing the fuss that would have ensued had she known his intentions, he had just left the flat as usual. For once she was not going to dictate to him; with the coming of war he had returned to his senses and regretted bitterly the long unhealed breach between himself and his mother. It was late as he breasted the last rise and swung in through the gate-tower onto the gravel in front of the dear old house. It was as if the old house cried out to him in welcome. Jumping out of the car, he strode to the door and jerked the bell.

'What's that?' Sarah looked up from her book.

'The front door, I think, Morpeth will go,' remarked Charles. 'I wonder who it can be at this hour?'

'Good evening, Master Duncan. May I say how pleased we are to see you.' Morpeth had succeeded Buttermere many years before and had known Duncan all his life. 'Your mother, and aunt and uncle, are in the long drawing-room. Have you eaten, or may I fetch you something?'

'No thanks, I stopped on my way down for a bite. Don't bother, I'll find my own way. It's good to see you again, though.' Swiftly, he strode down the hall and flung open the door. His voice had preceded him; they all thought they were dreaming. It was Emily, facing the door, who saw him first. She could just stare, then, blinking, she leapt to her feet, tears streaming down her face. With one stride, Duncan was across the room and had enfolded his mother in his strong arms.

'Mother, don't. I'm home now. I'm sorry, truly sorry.' He could say no more.

Charles, looking from his sister to Emily, cleared his throat and remarked to the room at large.

'Well, well, this calls for a celebration! – get the drinks, my boy.'

Duncan turned grinning and, opening the door, nearly bumped into Morpeth.

'Good evening, sir. Thought you might be requiring this, seeing as how Master Duncan has arrived.'

'Thank you, Morpeth.' Charles heaved himself out of his chair.

Duncan's reunion was all too short. Within forty-eight hours he had gone, posted overseas with his regiment. Emily bore up remarkably well, thankful to have had the chance to see her son. Far into the night they talked – there had been so much to say. Little Anne was now four and growing fast, while young Giles had celebrated his second birthday. They were both in Yorkshire with Caroline's parents and a nanny, while, for the present, Caroline was remaining in London, but would go north when he left, for to her disgust and annoyance, she was expecting another child.

Faced with the many problems that the outbreak of war brought in its wake, Charles' thoughts were turned to see how best he could help, and decided to hand his home over to a school. All over the country, they were pouring out of the towns to the safety of the countryside. The estate would continue to run itself, and he could easily keep an eye on it from another house. With the first mention of war, the Dower House had become vacant, its tenants having left on the first boat for Canada, much to the disgust of the local inhabitants. The move was easy; both houses were fully furnished, so they only had to move their personal belongings, the rest remained.

Harriet, hearing of her brother's decision, stepped in and took a hand. Her long family had grown up and married and in turn had had families of their own. Even now, her granddaughter's school was looking for an escape from their south London home. Already it had had one direct hit and they feared for more. London was no longer safe.

Delighted at the offer, the school moved down early in 1940, and their arrival coincided with the awaited announcement in *The Times* – another daughter. As before, never a word from Caroline. Emily had grown accustomed to it now, but it still hurt. She wondered what the little girl would be called and what they all looked like now.

Chapter XIV

'Nanny, where's Mummy?' asked Anne, kicking away at a stone in the river. The May sunshine shone down on the brownish green of the young heather, and for miles around the war seemed very far away. Wandering its leisurely and slightly lazy way down through the dales, the river rippled over the stony river-bed to where the ford, with its harder, smoother surface, was marked by a line of stepping stones. A wonderful playground for children! Today, down by its edge played three small children under the watchful eye of their ageing nanny. It was a favourite haunt of theirs and they often brought their tea down to the water's edge on nice days.

Little Anne, now seven, was puzzled. For two long years they had been living in a small cottage tucked away on the Yorkshire Moors. And every day, during the termtime, she and her five-year-old brother Giles would set off to the far side of the village to attend a dame school. It was a good mile from their cottage to the house where they had their lessons and the landmarks soon became familiar. First the red pillar box on the cross-roads by the village school and then the dip. This, when she was allowed to ride her fairy-cycle, was the greatest fun, for it was a wonderful feeling to sail down the steep slope and up the far side, as fast as she could go. But on school days, she had to walk. At the top of the dip, the village green and its pond were the next landmarks to come in sight. Away to the left beyond the green, the village shop looked out over its peaceful surroundings. Leaving this exciting place on their left, the two children would trot on up the long straight road towards the moorland that rose steeply at the end of the village and sheltered their small school from the wind

104

that swept in off the barren lands that stretched for miles.

Caroline, deadly jealous of Duncan's mother, had succeeded in her ardent desire to alienate her husband from his own family. She hated her mother-in-law with the bitter loathing that comes when two dominant characters meet and clash. With the advent of every child, the loathing grew. They hampered her activities and spoilt her figure, a figure of which she was justly proud. Mary, born three years after Giles, had been the last straw. She had not wanted another child, any more than she had wanted the first two, and this, coupled with the discovery that Duncan, without a word to her, had been down to his home to see his mother, together with the outbreak of war, had given her a bitter sense of grievance towards her children. To her small, petty mind, they stood for all that had wronged her in the world. With Duncan's swift departure for the battlefields of Europe, she had retired to her parents' home in a huff, to await the arrival of her unwanted child. She never let these things worry her, and within three months of Mary's arrival she had returned south in righteous patriotism to join the ATS, excellent in itself, but not in motive. Before long she had gained the coveted job of driving a staff car and was content. She liked the life, and the uniform suited her. There was excitement, and this, together with people to admire her, which she craved most of all and without which she could not live, meant she had a life that might have been made for her.

As the days and months drifted into years, Nanny Brandon wished wholeheartedly that her mistress would either write, or, better still, come and see her children. She knew this to be possible, and could not understand why she never came. Duncan, on the other hand, who loved his children, did write and never failed to remember their birthdays and Christmas; but it was Caroline they missed, for her absence bewildered them, especially Anne, who was old enough to realize what was going on.

If Nanny was worried now, it was nothing to her worry the previous summer, with the whole responsibility of the children on her hands. With the coming of summer, the peace of the moor had been shattered by the arrival of a batch of evacuees from an industrial town in the north – an unruly bunch of varying ages, accompanied by a master.

Their impact had had startling effect. Barely forty-eight hours had elapsed before some enterprising member of the party, deeming lessons and a guardian unnecessary to their livelihood, had locked the unfortunate person in the 'smallest room in the school', and left him to stew over the weekend, where, luckily for him, some passer-by heard his cries for help and released him before any damage to his health had been done! Needless to say, before long, this batch of youngsters were terrorizing the whole neighbourhood.

Anne, walking home one day alone with her school-books, and swinging her gas-mask by its long leather handle, looked up to hear a loud cowboy war-whoop. Startled, she saw on the far side of the dip, a large group of bigger children rise up like Highlanders from the heather in the days of the '45. Terrified, she watched them cover the intervening terrain and swarm, yelling and whooping, up the nearest slope towards her and the village. As the menacing mob advanced, Anne retreated step by step into the corner by the boundary wall of the big house that overlooked the dip. Within seconds, the first bully had arrived on the scene to encounter a small spitfire. Manfully swinging her gas-mask case, Anne beat off the attack, flaying their legs unmercifully, as reinforcements hurried up to help the early arrivals. Anne, like a tiger-cub at bay, fought back valiantly. Then one boy drew a knife and threatened the small girl, but still she fought on – the gas-mask doing far greater service than it was ever visualised for. Step by step, Anne was forced to give ground, then the cold hard stone wall brushed unyieldingly against her thin bare legs. In an instant, she had turned and was desperately trying to climb the high barricading wall that rose perpendicularly above her head. Across the valley, her loud and lusty screams, for she was a true Ravensworth, rang out to reach Nanny in their cottage. Dropping all, the old lady started to run as fast as her tired legs would carry her. Down the lane and across the cross-roads she trundled at full speed. The sight that met her weary grey eyes sent a cold tingle down her spine. For across the valley, she could just pick out her little Anne desperately climbing the wall, turning every now and then and flaying her aggressors as she went, with her trusty friend. She was a tough little monkey, when driven to it, and not easily daunted. Nanny, nearly frantic with worry, tore on down the hill and up the far side. But long before she had reached Anne, a tall, slightly bent man came striding down the road. His deep voice gave Anne reassurance and drove terror into the hearts of the bullies, who with one accord fell back and vanished.

'Come, my child, they won't hurt you now.' Strong hands lifted Anne down from the wall, where she had just reached the top.

'Thank . . . you.' Anne's voice was unsteady now that the danger had gone, and she felt unaccountably frightened. It was silly – but a fact. 'I was trying to climb in. Sorry if it was your garden, but they were stronger than me.' The old man patted her on the shoulder and taking her hand, looked round to see if she had anyone with her before setting off towards her home.

'That's all right. Little girls shouldn't be alone, though. Where's your companion?' His voice was kind, and Anne, who used to go to school each day with a friend from next door, replied quickly,

'Jane's ill, so I had to come alone. It's not far, I've only got to go to the cottages on the far side. I'm six. Nanny is busy, she's got Giles and Mary to look after.' Chattering away, Anne allowed herself to be led off towards her home. Before they had reached the bottom, Nanny, puffing her way up towards them, was thankful beyond words to see her Anne safe, and gathering the little girl to her ample person, thanked the old man profusely. After that, every day, Anne would find the old man waiting for her outside his gate. He had become the small girls' self-appointed guardian and would see them both safely home, or failing himself, someone else would always bring the children back. So within a short time, the bullies owned defeat, and except on rare occasions, when they would come to the cluster of cottages on the hill and bait the children playing there, they became little trouble. Even so, Nanny kept a watchful eye on her three charges, and seldom let them wander far from home without her.

With the bullies subdued, the summer passed peacefully, until one night the steady drone of planes could be heard high in the night sky. A long way off, the sirens screamed out their eerie wail in the big towns many miles off across the moors. Anne opened her eyes and lay listening. Nearer and nearer they zoomed, then, Bump! Bump! Bump! What was that? Scrambling to her window, she looked out across the river, where a small glow lit the sky. It grew and grew. Rushing into her room, Nanny whipped the small girl from her bed and bore her off downstairs and pushed her under the divan in the sitting room along with Giles and baby Mary. The lightly built house rocked on its foundations as bomb followed bomb in ever increasing numbers. Eventually, after what seemed like hours, the planes left and all was once more quiet. Outside, the moor burnt. Within its thick heather, the bombs lay waiting – alive and dangerous – everywhere.

The next night, the process was repeated. The only difference was that instead of the young Ravensworths 'going to ground', they sat up in the sitting-room and drank cocoa. By now the smell of burning was filling the night air and the whole atmosphere reeked of burning peat. Once again, the raid over, they returned to bed. To poor Nanny's horror, the third night brought a repetition of the previous two. This time it differed only that, instead of staying indoors, they all stood on the back doorstep and watched the bombs falling from the sky to drop less than a mile away in the heather across the river. With every bomb that fell, the fire grew, till sixteen square miles of burning peat covered the moorland that stretched out before them. Overhead, still the planes droned on. With every bump, the thin walled little cottage rocked and shook on its none too strong foundations. Those three nights, along with a certain one earlier in the year when they had had to travel to Whitby over the moor in the middle of the night with planes droning steadily overhead on their way to visit the big industrial towns of the north, would remain with Nanny for a long time. Oddly enough, after the first frightening night, the children had enjoyed their night vigils; they were exciting! Now the only fear that lurked was that of the risk of showing a light during the hours of black-out, for the fire had been started by a tiny glow on the moor, a decoy to draw off the bombers from their main targets. What was so remarkable about the whole show, and made it possible to look back on it without regret or sorrow, was the fact that not one person or thing lost its life; the only thing that was hit at all was an old cart-horse stable right out in the middle of nowhere, and even then, the cart-horse was not said to be at home but sadly he had been. Nevertheless, Nanny had had enough and had no wish for a repeat this summer; all she wanted was for the children's mother to come and see them.

Another year and a half passed but still there was no sign of Caroline. Nanny was getting anxious. Anne, the eldest and the only one really to remember her mother, was beginning to suffer. The once bright child was becoming very quiet and solemn, and after school, would sit for hours on end staring into space. Everywhere, children were talking about their parents and their achievements. Anne, a truthful child at heart, could not bring herself to make up stories about hers, for it was over six months since they had had news of Duncan. What could she say? She knew Daddy was fighting – but where? What doing? Anne knew not.

Then just before Christmas, Nanny saw the announcement she had expected and dreaded for so long.

'RAVENSWORTH. Major John Duncan Ravensworth, MC, of . . . Regiment. Killed in action. November 30th, 1943.' It was a short announcement, but it told her all she needed to know. She had been fond of Duncan and knew that six months before he had been taken prisoner and then escaped to rejoin his regiment a few months later – only for this. It was sad and the children must be told, but until their mother gave the word, she could but wait. But this was not for long. Three days later a battered Caroline at last returned to her children. For the next week they hardly saw her. In her own way, Caroline had loved Duncan and his death, even after so long away from her, came as no less a blow, and she kept to her room, a room that until her arrival had been Nanny's. Now Nanny shared Mary's tiny room and waited for her mistress to express her wishes. On the fifth day, Caroline came down to the sitting room to find her children playing Snakes-and-Ladders before a small log fire. Hearing footsteps, three small strangers looked up, their long period of waiting over, with a mixture of shyness and excitement. Wonderment was written large on their small faces. With the expectant gaze of small children, they fixed their eyes on their mother's face. In the background, Nanny hovered anxiously. The silence was terrible and save for a wind whistling round the back of the cottage and howling at intervals, not a sound could be heard. Caroline, her usual sang-froid returned, gazed back with her cold, blue eyes. Looking at her three children – eight – six and little Mary who would be four the following spring, she hardly smiled. Then, as if to throw away her last link with the family she had never wanted, she spoke with a voice like an iceberg.

'Well, children. How are you?' She paused; but they were silent. Their whole world had crumbled. They could sense that they were no longer wanted. Caroline continued in her same brutal fashion. 'I'm afraid I've got bad news for you. Your father is dead.'

These words, uttered with such coldness, knocked the very cornerstone of their existence from under them, and none of them even cried. They were too stunned and shattered even to take in fully what their mother was saying.

'Why, oh why,' thought Anne to herself, 'didn't Nanny tell us? She must have known.'

True, Nanny had known and would have told them, had not Caroline forbidden her. Caroline reserved that right for herself.

Their mother's voice continued to drone on through the wilderness.

'I have decided to close this cottage and send you all to school. It will be much the best thing, as I am busy and my parents need Nanny to help them. At your father's request, I am sending you to schools of his choice. Anne, you are going to a Convent where one of your cousins went. Mary will go with you; they've agreed to take her. Giles, you are too old to go with your sisters, so you will go to your father's old prep school. Where, no doubt, you will all be happy. So I will say good-bye.' With these final words she swept out of the room, and out of the lives of her children forever.

Chapter XV

Caroline's fateful words took a long time to sink into the young minds of her children. To them, it was like living in a bad dream – a card-house they had built laboriously with infinite care and concentration, only to see it blown down, by a puff of wind, before their eyes; but unlike a card-house, they could never re-build it.

December gave way to the New Year and at the beginning of the second week in January, they left the cottage and found themselves, bewildered and mystified, sitting in a train roaring south into the unknown. It was late when at last they arrived at King's Cross. Throughout the long and endless journey from the north, food had been unobtainable. Tired, hungry, and worn out to the point of collapse, they stumbled from the train. Giles, nearly asleep on his feet, stepped back and completed a backwards somersault over a stationary line of trucks on the platform. It was Anne who hurried forward to pick up her small brother and dust him down.

'It's all right, Giles, we won't be long now. Nanny says we're nearly there.' Looking across at Mary, sleeping the sleep of the exhausted in Nanny's arms, Anne had her responsibility as the eldest brought home to her, as she took her brother's hand and prepared to follow. They were so small and vulnerable, and Anne felt very inadequate and young to cope with what lay ahead. Would this nightmare never end?

A miserable Anne, two days later, found herself dressed in her new dark blue uniform, gloomily surveying a large and imposing house. Mary, beyond whose comprehension the whole affair was, clutched tightly at her sister's hand; as long as she had Anne, she felt safe. Slowly, Anne let her gaze wander in wonderment up across the

111

windows and along the house till she was gazing, not at the house, but at the wide acres of the park and away to the lake. As she stood, an odd feeling of calm and security descended over her for the first time in her life. It was as if she had come home. Unaccountably, tears ran down her thin face and fell on the gravel at her feet.

Several weeks passed before Anne began to settle in her new surroundings. Mary, on the other hand, still little more than a baby, took it all much more for granted. She still had Anne and therefore security, for after all, she had never known her parents. For Anne, her father's pet, it was different; she had known and loved her father and her loss was all the greater. Above all, she missed Giles. Their childish letters to one another were a poor substitute for each other's company.

Feeling particularly lonely and homesick one day, Anne crept away from her class in the junior school, and wandered off towards the attics. Here, in a dark corner by the back stairs, she sat down and buried her face in her small hands and let the silent sobs that were pent up within her taut little body shake her slender frame. How long she sat there, Anne knew not! The other children, meaning to be kind, had been asking her about her family and why the house bore the same name as herself. Anne, unable to answer the question that she herself had thought odd and then dismissed as one of those things that had no answer, had stuck it as long as possible, and then slipped away to the comfort and seclusion of her hiding place. She hated being asked about her family and home – she had no home and no father, only a mother who did not want her.

Prudence, passing swiftly along the passage to the Chapel over the stables in search of one of the nuns, heard muffled sobs and went to investigate.

'Why, what's the matter?' An arm went round the little girl huddled in the corner. The voice was kind.

'Nothing.' Anne would rather have died than been found crying.

'Nothing? But there must be. What's your name? You must be new, aren't you?'

'Yes; I'm Anne.'

'Anne. Anne who?' There was something gentle in the older girl that made Anne come out of her shell and shyly she looked up through blurred eyes.

'Anne Ravensworth; I came this term with my younger sister Mary.'

'Good heavens! Are you a Ravensworth? Who's your father?'

Somehow, Anne, who had hated being questioned by her friends, found herself readily answering this tall, kind girl that sat on the stairs beside her.

'He's dead. He was Major Duncan Ravensworth, and he was killed just before Christmas.' Anne gulped. 'Mother doesn't want us any more, so we've been sent here, and my brother Giles to another school.'

Prudence did not know what to say to this. Here was a Ravensworth, unknowingly, seemingly, in her own home. With care she questioned the little girl further.

'What other relations have you, Anne?'

Anne shook her head.

'None, only my grandparents in Yorkshire, but they don't want us children. We're a nuisance to them. I once asked if our father had any relations, but Nanny merely changed the subject, which meant that Mummy had forbidden her to tell us. She was like that. But I don't expect there are any relations, not ones that would want us.'

Prudence smiled to herself; Anne had a big surprise awaiting her. By degrees she extracted the whole story from the little girl, keeping her own identity to herself, Anne was in awe of the senior school, and this one had a wide blue ribbon lying across her shoulder and hanging down her left side, so she never dreamt of asking her, though she did seem to know a lot about the family!

'Anne, my dear, if you are feeling up to facing the others now, I think it would be wise for you to go back, or you will be missed. As it is, no one need know where you have been, but promise me you will never do it again. If you want anything, at any time, come and find me. Come, I'm going past the junior school myself, so we can go together. Ready?' Prudence helped the smaller girl to her feet and taking the small cold hand in hers led her off towards her own classroom.

That evening after supper, Prudence caught the eye of the head-girl as she made her rounds with her list for those who wished to see the Mistress General.

'What? You?' Catherine raised her eyebrows and made a grimace at her friend. Prudence was not a usual visitor to that 'Holy of Holies'.

'Good evening, Mother.' Prudence quietly shut the door and crossed the oak panelled room. Curtsying, she waited by the headmistress's desk.

'Good evening, Prudence. What brings you here? Sit down, my dear.'

It was a kindly smile that greeted the tall, fair haired girl, with the odd grey-green eyes.

'I've come, Mother, about little Anne Ravensworth, the new girl.'

With care, Prudence went on to unfold Anne's story. She had given a great deal of thought to what Anne had told her, and was puzzled.

'She must be my cousin, Mother. Her father asked that she should come here because one of his cousins had been here; well, I'm that cousin, so she must be Aunt Emily's grandchild. I know there was some upset over Cousin Duncan's marriage, but Aunt Emily seldom speaks of it, so I don't know the full story. Has Aunt said anything to you about her grand-daughters coming here?' Prudence looked anxiously across at her headmistress.

'No, Prudence, but then your aunt only returned late last night from your mother's place, and I haven't had time to go and see her yet. The name Ravensworth had struck me as odd, but then I don't know a great deal about your family. I was only asked if I would take the children for the war, as their mother was in the ATS, and could not cope with them. I had no idea that she had left them.'

'Yes, that sounds very like Cousin Caroline, from the little my mother has let drop, when she has been at the Dower House. Aunt Sarah is a little more outspoken. Please, may I go down to see Aunt Emily tomorrow. I'm convinced she's Anne's grandmother.'

'Certainly, my dear, go after lunch.'

For a while, Prudence Lavenham, whose father Harry Lavenham had married a Catholic, an old girl of the school, and the Mistress General talked of both Anne and little Mary, and of other topics of interest in the school. Then came the signal for Prudence to leave. It was time for Evening Prayers, and she would have to join the rest of

114

the school in the long corridor on the first floor, where, every night, they assembled before retiring to bed.

'Good-night, my child and God bless you.'

Snow had been falling for two days now and lay thick as Prudence strode with purpose through the park towards the village the following day after lunch. Hockey and netball were off, so in the park, parties of small girls raced and played, their happy laughter filling the crisp February air as it echoed off the surrounding hills and filled the valleys. Away in the distance, Prudence saw Anne racing with her classmates, and was thankful. In another day or two, Prudence hoped the lake would be frozen enough for skating, but in the meantime it was forbidden territory!

'Come in.' Emily's voice called through the hall from the dining room, where she was seated at the table writing letters.

'Hello, Aunt Emily. It's only me.' Prudence threw off her coat and unwound her long school scarf from her throat. 'Guess what!'

'Can't, but come and get warm, my dear; not that there's much fire. That school of yours seems to need so much wood to keep you warm!' Emily was ageing gracefully. She was still a remarkably good looking woman, and thought, not for the first time, how very like her grandmother Prudence was becoming. She had the same kindness as Harriet had had when Emily had first met her all those years ago. With a smile she continued, 'Uncle Charles and Aunt Sarah are out. Did you want to see them?'

'No, Aunt Emily, it's you I've come to see.' Prudence paused. She knew the subject of Cousin Duncan was tricky, and wondered how best to start. Realizing it must be done, she took a deep breath and looking straight at her aunt went on, 'We have two little girls up at the school, Anne and Mary Ravensworth.' Emily looked up startled. 'They came while you were with my mother. The Mistress General said I might come down; she never guessed for a moment that you were unaware that they were here. Have I done right? I've said nothing to Anne yet, she's a darling, you'll love her, and Mary.'

'Yes, my darling, you've just done the best thing you've ever done in your life. You don't know what this means to me, or will mean to them.' Emily, tears running unconstrained down her face, hugged

115

her niece. She could hardly believe it was true. Bless Duncan for doing what little he could; she only hoped it was not too late, for Prudence's story was almost unbelievable. It was so cold-blooded and heartless.

Sunday at last arrived and two nervous little girls waited with Prudence on the door step of the Dower House. Bidding her aunt farewell, Prudence had lost no time in seeking out their headmistress, to tell her the good news and get her blessing to tell Anne. The little girl's delight knew no bounds. After all, out of the blue, she too had relations, and one of them was right there in the school. It was wonderful. In fact, she and Mary had hundreds of relations! To the two unwanted little girls, it had opened up another world – a world which the other children could understand. Even so, they were rather shy at the prospect of meeting their grandmother, for grandmothers, to them, were heartless, cruel people that, in real life, were extremely like those in their fairy books! Within seconds of ringing the bell, the door flew open and Anne and Mary found themselves enfolded in a warm embrace – an embrace equal to nothing they had experienced before.

'Darlings,' Emily could hardly speak for happiness. The children too, were speechless. Anne at last felt safe. She was loved. She was wanted. What bliss! It would be a long time though before she could forget. Her mother's callousness had bitten too deep.

Tea that afternoon was certainly a bright and cheerful meal. Shortly after they had started, Uncle Charles and Aunt Sarah came in, to the delight of the little girls. So, here, at long last, were their great-nieces. Emily's face reflected their own feelings. If the children were pleased to have found their family, it was only equalled by their family's pleasure at having found them.

Emily, in her downright manner, had little doubt in her own mind as to the children's future. Their holidays were to be spent with her at the Dower House – from now on her home was their home, But for the time being they would remain as boarders, but could come home at week-ends if they wanted to. In this way they would have a chance to settle, for a day child in a boarding school is as out of things as a boarder at a day school. What they needed now was security, and this was what they would have at all costs. Next week-end would see all three of them together, for Emily had already arranged to have Giles home for the whole week-end, so that he could see his sisters, who would be joining him at the Dower House.

Chapter XVI

Anne, for the first time since her father had gone away, had at last found a reason for living. Her whole life had been transformed, and life had taken on a new and shining complexion. For days she went round the school in a dream, but knowing the reason, no one cared, least of all the nuns, who were sweetness itself to the two small girls.

Her grandmother, in the meantime, never one to dawdle at the best of times when an important issue was at stake, had taken matters into her own very capable hands. Hardly had she kissed the girls goodbye and watched them all off on their way back to the school than she had closed the front door with purpose and retreated to her desk. For a few minutes she sat in silence; the Dower House seemed to hold its breath awaiting her next move – it had seen so much Ravensworth history made under its roof and tonight was no exception. Drawing a headed sheet of paper from the rack, she set about the grim task of writing to her daughter-in-law. In a few well chosen words she gave Caroline some home truths about herself that should have made her quake, for Emily took almost sadistic pleasure in not pulling her punches. Sarah looking into the room as Emily worked, smiled to herself.

'What, writing to Caroline?'

'Why yes, but how did you know?' asked Emily, surprised, looking up from her writing.

'By your face. You have your determined look; also I believe you are almost enjoying it, now you have the children safe. You've secretly been longing to do this for years, haven't you?'

Emily gracefully inclined her head and gave Sarah a wry smile, a

118

twinkle lurking in the depths of her dark eyes.

'Well, yes, I suppose I have.'

If Emily had expected a swift reply to her letter, it was not forthcoming. She was annoyed. She did not like being thwarted, especially by someone as cold-blooded as Caroline, and she was rapidly growing impatient. The planned week-end to reunite the family had been a great success. Giles had been thrilled to find he had a real home after all. Now he looked forward to his holidays with eagerness and expectancy, where before there had been an empty, lonely feeling. He was content enough at school, as he had one or two other boys of his own age, but he missed his sisters and the prospect of remaining at school for the holidays had been dismal to the extreme. Now that was all different – he had the Dower House and Granny to go home to, not to mention an uncle and aunt as well as his sisters.

February was running out and still no word from Caroline. Sarah, casting her eye down the section of the paper she liked best, let out an exclamation and passed the paper across to Emily with a wry smile.

'Here, read this.'

Emily's experienced eye quickly alighted on the brief announcement. 'CARSON-RAVENSWORTH. The marriage took place quietly in London recently of Paul Carson of Illinois, USA and Caroline (née Brandon) widow of Major J.D. Ravensworth, MC.'

'Well, she's not wasted much time!' Emily remarked cuttingly as she handed back the paper.

'No. Now what?' asked Sarah, watching her sister-in-law intently. She knew that look on Emily's face only too well. Emily was on the warpath! Between pursed lips, with grim determination, Emily stared into the flickering flames.

'They're mine now.' So quietly were these words uttered that Sarah hardly heard them.

Duncan, anxious about his children's future should he get killed, had requested in his will that should Caroline ever re-marry, then, if possible, the children were to be given into the guardianship of his own mother, providing Caroline agreed. For, knowing his wife, he realized that she would not want to be burdened with his children, once he had gone! How right he had been. Now, thanks to Prudence, their future was secure. No longer would they want for a home. Emily, receiving a reply at long last, shortly after the announcement, gave a satisfied chuckle. She had won that rubber and Anne, Giles and Mary had nothing more to fear.

The children's school days were the same as any other normal child brought up at a boarding school during wartime. It was a happy life, and during their holidays, they roamed the countryside – living the life they enjoyed: riding and walking, swimming in the summer and bicycling miles along the country lanes around Ravensworth. Charles once more held out the hand of father to these children and did his best to do for them what he had done for their father in his childhood. They quickly found an ally and friend in their uncle, and loved nothing more than to be allowed to go round the estate with him. The Dower House, too, became a gay, cheerful place, as the younger generation started to come for visits, filling the old house with laughter. The young Ravensworths were lucky in one thing; Harriet's youngest daughter Elizabeth, who had married Frank Matlock in the early thirties, had two children about their own age, and they loved nothing better than their visits to the old rambling farmhouse on the fringe of the South Downs. They always had so much to do and see around them that there was seldom a dull moment. On their first visit, during the summer of 1944, they had the mixed excitement of seeing their first doodle-bug. Off for the afternoon on their bikes, Anne and Giles were cycling along with Margaret and Jack when all of a sudden Jack braked hard and shouted to the others.

'Silence! What's that?' Like lightning, born of much practice, he and his sister were off their bikes, closely followed by Anne and Giles. Overhead, in the distance, the steady drone of an engine reached their straining ears. Then it stopped. 'Down, everyone, in the ditch,' shouted Jack, the eldest of the party, pulling Anne down behind him as he spoke and lying on her and Giles. Hardly had they made the cover of the ditch than into view over the hedge came the flaming monster, swooping relentlessly down on them. 'One – two – three – four – . . . forty-one . . . fifty – fifty-one – . . . fifty-nine . . .' Jack was counting away the seconds from the time the engine had cut. The thing was roaring right over their heads now, low and fearsome. One more second and it would be down! Quickly they said their prayers and stole a peep between their fingers. Oddly enough, fear was not a companion today, though they all knew enough of doodle-bugs to realize that when the engine cut out, there were only sixty short seconds before it would crash and burn to bits wherever it landed. And in those sixty seconds it would cover just one mile, like a burning inferno. Already they had watched one being escorted over the woods that surrounded the house and then shot up by the escorting Spitfires – only to crash a mile away in a field, where they found it two days later and collected a piece of the fuselage as a war trophy, with childish glee. Windows, too, blew in with the greatest of ease. If one crashed in the neighbourhood now, they were facing death, as near as they had ever faced it. But somehow, they knew they would be safe. Behind them, across the road, lay their abandoned bikes, where they had dropped them in their hurry to seek the safety of the ditch. Within seconds of first seeing the monster, the big crash echoed across the lonely countryside. It was down – one field from where the children lay! They were safe despite exceeding the sixty seconds!.

'Phew! that one was a near thing!' remarked Jack as he scrambled out and gave the others a hand. 'All right?'

'Yes thanks.' They were laughing now, as they climbed back onto their bikes and rode off as if nothing unusual had happened!

The months passed and the war progressed, and with the advent of the New Year, things began to look more heartening. The long awaited end was nigh. By the beginning of May it was obvious that they had not long to wait for the final word. At any rate in Germany, it would soon be all over.

Down in the park, on the far side of the lake, the whole school, with Sir Charles' full permission, began to build a monster bonfire that towered towards the sky, while every night, up at the house after supper, the school gathered on the steps that led to the lawns from what had been the long drawing-room and listened, with the Mistress General, for Winston Churchill and the longed for news. Would it ever come? The days seemed endless – but still they waited. Then, just as the waiting became unbearable – it came. The war was over. They were at peace. On the night of 8th May the fire went up. What a day it had been! What rejoicing, and how they sang and danced long into the night! Bedtime was waived that night, till the last of the flickering flames had died away. Over the rejoicing world, the only cloud that still remained was the cloud that shrouded the Far East. The Japanese were fighting to the bitter end. But to everyone's relief, that, too, lifted at the end of August. England was at peace – or was she?

The strain of the long years of war had proved a drain on Charles. No longer a young man, he had begun to feel his age long before the war had broken out, and by the end he was tired. Early one morning, as the autumn was beginning to tinge the woods and park with its changing colours and the leaves slowly drifted down from the tall trees to carpet the ground beneath in a rich bronze, the Towers lost yet another Master. Charles had died of a heart attack shortly before his eighty-first birthday, and for miles around he was mourned by all who had known and respected him.

The long drawn out weeks that followed Charles' death were anxious ones for his family. A poser now faced the estate – who was the heir? Who indeed? And where in this wide world lived James? Legally he was his brother's heir. But how to trace him, that was the big problem.

'Sarah, can't you find anything that might give us a clue in those letters?' Emily and Sarah were once again going through old Sir Giles' papers – papers that had been sorted many times before during the previous months since Charles' death.

'No. The Trustees wrote today, too, saying they've drawn a blank in the only address we did find. It's certainly a problem.'

And it went on as the months drifted by and yet another new year began in much the same manner.

For the school, too, Sir Charles' death had set a problem. To return to London was out of the question. Their building had suffered three direct hits during the blitz, and to continue at the Towers was unpractical, for the old house was too small to accommodate the school in peacetime and they wished to be nearer London and their sister schools in the South. Taking all these matters into consideration, the Reverend Mother set off on her travels to find a new home for the school. After many disappointments she came across the ideal place nestling in a fold of the North Downs within reach of London and the other schools, and at the same time in the country with ample room for expansion. So, early the following July, the school broke up for the summer holidays and left the Towers for the last time; next term they would be many miles away, and about to make history in the life of the school. For many, it was a sad move. Their wartime home had been a happy one, and they had grown to love the old house, complete still with all its furniture and paintings, and surrounded by its rolling parklands. To those who had loved the country, it had offered freedom and peaceful happiness.

The new house was exciting. Everywhere, building was in progress and by degrees, under their very eyes, it took shape, with the gymnasium, then the brand-new science wing and all the things the Towers had been unable to provide and which made the move acceptable. It opened up new and exciting ventures.

For Anne and Mary, this was not the only move that year, for at Christmas they came home, not to the Dower House, but to another, smaller house on Harriet's estate. With grave misgivings and heavy hearts, Emily and Sarah had made up their minds.

'It's no good, Emily,' Sarah remarked shortly after the girls had gone back for the winter term and the house was empty again, 'we can't stay.'

'I know, we've stuck it for a year and the trustees are being beastly; we can't call our souls our own any more.'

'Yes, I realize that and I think we had better accept Harriet's offer and leave here till the settlement is made and we know where we stand with the trust and who the estate belongs to now.'

Neither old lady was the type to bow gracefully to interfering trustees for their smallest wish, and the move was imperative, if peace was to reign. One day, maybe, they could return to Ravensworth, but in the meantime they would be better off with Harriet.

Naturally they all missed the Towers and the Dower House, but Harriet was, as ever, kind and considerate. She knew what a wrench it was for her sister and Emily to leave their native Cotswolds and went out of her way to help them settle in the small Sussex farmhouse a couple of miles from her own home. It was a pretty house and had once been part of a small farm, the land of which David had taken into the home farm to make it a workable proposition. David and Harriet had been delighted to let Sarah and Emily have the house, and their company went a long way to compensate them for the loss of their old home and friends, and to help them make new ones, for after all, they had been at Ravensworth for over half a century.

Chapter XVII

'Hallo, Bill, what now?' Giles watched his friend wriggle from under his old jalopy. Giles was now doing his National Service and had driven over to see an old school friend who was undergoing training at an air station in the Cotswolds, not far from where he himself was stationed on the Wiltshire Downs.

'Oh, hallo, Giles! Just finished. Care to come for a spin? Going to try the old girl now and see what happens.' Bill's round cheerful face was smeared with oil, giving him a peculiar expression, reminiscent of a sleek tabby cat.

'OK. Anywhere in particular?'

'No.' Bill wiped off the oil on a once clean handkerchief, which for the last half hour had been doing duty as an oil rag! 'I'm easy.'

Within a quarter of an hour they were both speeding northwards, to the best of the old car's ability. It was nearly ten years since Giles had last passed along the country lanes through which they now travelled. Then he had been only nine, now he was eighteen – school was behind him. The pale March sun shone through the clouds that fled across the sky with great rapidity. Giles gave a contented sigh of pleasure. It was good to be alive. In his lean body, every nerve ached towards his reunion with his old home which he had loved so dearly.

Approaching Ravensworth from the south, they swung off into the narrow lane that led to the main gates to the park. Ahead lay the high stone pillars capped with their round balls of Cotswold stone. How well he remembered it as if it were only yesterday! The drive, though, seemed even longer than usual as they bumped their way up it from pot-hole to pot-hole.

'Hi! where the hell are you bringing me?' laughed Bill, as they hit a larger than usual hole. With every bump, they left their seats, only to return in time for the next.

'This was the front drive,' remarked Giles dubiously, 'I know it was. Uncle Charles used to tell me all about the place when I was small. We lived in the Dower House then, down in the village.'

At long last the lake and river came in sight, and away across the hill, the dear old gate-tower and house itself.

'There you are.' There was pride in Giles' voice that he could not suppress – just pride, Bill realized that.

Pulling up on the grass covered gravel a few moments later, Giles got his first shock. He knew the place had stood empty for a long time; but beyond that, he had not thought what it would have meant to the place. Least of all had it ever dawned on him that the place he had loved so dearly could have deteriorated into its present deplorable state. Everywhere the story was the same: broken windows, doors swinging on loose hinges. Pushing one door, Giles and Bill squeezed through and wandered aimlessly through the desolate rooms. It was hard now to believe, as they knew that when the school left it had been handed over in spotless condition and first class order. Not a pin had been out of place when the key had been turned in the lock; now the whole place was just rotting. A hurried scuffle behind the wainscoting told of an unwanted inhabitant, and the mass of cobwebs told of others.

'Ough, let's get out of this. I can't bear it,' said Giles, turning to Bill as they reached the kitchens. Here the house became bleak beyond belief. Once outside, Giles spoke again. 'You would never think this had once been a beautiful place. I never lived in it myself, but I was often brought over in the holidays.'

The Dower House proved a much more heartening sight. It was still inhabited and curtains showed from the windows, so instead of stopping, they swung the car round and headed south down the valley towards Cirencester.

On the road home, Giles was strangely silent, Bill knew what a shock his friend had received and respected his silence, and drove on as fast as the old car would comfortably go.

'Thanks, Bill. I'll be ringing you.' Giles' mind was far away back in the hills from whence they had just come, as he stepped from Bill's car and, waving, crossed to his own. He even refused to join Bill for a drink, on the plea that he must get back, an unheard of thing for Giles.

Hardly had he reached his own quarters and sat down at his desk, than he whipped out a piece of paper and dashed off a hasty note.

'Dearest Anne – Must see you. Meet me Ravensworth Station next Sunday without fail. Urgent. With love, Giles. P.S. Don't tell Gran, just come. Explain then.'

Anne received this letter the following morning. Luckily for her she was alone when the post arrived or otherwise her gasp of surprise would have made Granny inquisitive. Emily was a remarkable old lady now, with her wits very much about her. It was not easy to pull the wool over Granny's eyes as well the children knew from past experience. At seventy-five, she was alert and active, and could easily have been taken for a woman several years younger. Slipping the letter into her pocket, Anne frowned.

'Now what does Giles want?' she muttered under her breath, as she pulled on her coat and went in search of Granny to say goodbye. Leaving school at seventeen, Anne had done a year at a secretarial college before returning to work in her uncle's estate office. Uncle David, getting on in years, had welcomed his niece's help and she found the work both interesting and absorbing. A quiet, shy girl, Anne preferred her own company to that of others, though at time she would surprise her friends by throwing back her head and roaring with laughter. In short, she was extremely unpredictable, for her early childhood had left its mark. Throughout her long schooldays she had been popular. Fair at work, good at games, she could be relied upon to do her best. Though not a Catholic, she had found it no handicap – she was one of many, and as the years drifted by she found her love of the Faith growing, till shortly before she left, she knew which road she wished to take and she and Mary were received into the Church in the new Chapel that had once been a cattle shed, a very appropriate setting. Though she and Mary had become Catholics, they were in the minority, as most of their non-Catholic contemporaries had left as they had come – non-Catholics. In their case, the loving kindness, after a stormy childhood, had drawn them into the fold. No pressure had ever been brought to bear upon them in any way. The decision was theirs and theirs alone, a decision that Giles, too, came to make of his own free will a few months after leaving school. Now all three were Catholics and in another month, at Easter, Emily too would be received. It was a day which Anne had prayed for for so long.

'So long, Gran, see you at lunchtime.' Anne kissed the slightly wrinkled cheek, hurried down the shallow steps and jumped into her small car. She was late and that would never do. All morning her mind kept wandering back to Giles' extremely brief letter. What on earth could he be up to now?

A week of high winds and lashing rain followed and Anne began to wonder if Sunday would ever come. Hurrying through her breakfast after early church, Anne ran upstairs to collect her coat and bag. Reaching the landing, she nearly collided with her grandmother.

'Sorry, Gran. Look, I'm just off. Expect me when you see me. I have to meet someone.' With a quick kiss, Anne slipped off down the stairs and out of the house, leaving her grandmother staring after her retreating back. Aunt Sarah was still in her room, so Anne had not had to run the gauntlet there, which had been fortunate, for Aunt Sarah was very swift to sense something strange and would question one unmercifully. Between them, Anne would never have escaped. As it was her grandmother's voice had faded on the breeze as she drove out of the drive and headed west.

'Now, what's she up to?' mused Emily, turning towards the dining room to finish her breakfast. Now she came to think of it, Anne had been hiding something all the week!

'Well done; I knew you would make it.' Giles was waiting by his car as Anne drove up. It had taken her just four hours to reach Ravensworth. The Sunday traffic was fairly heavy and she had been held up on the Guildford by-pass.

'Now then, brother. What's all this about?' Anne pulled the crumpled letter from her pocket as she spoke.

Giles grinned at his sister and with his disarming smile replied. 'Jump in, sister, and I'll explain.'

Sitting side by side in Giles' car, they drank scalding coffee out of a flask that Anne had brought along with her, and munched biscuits. Slowly, between mouthfuls, Giles unfolded his plans for their future. Anne, excited to be back at Ravensworth, listened enthralled.

'Come, we'll drive up to the Towers now, and you can see for yourself.'

Leaving Anne's little car in the station yard, Giles swung his out of the station and headed along familiar roads to their old home. If Giles had been shocked, it was nothing to the shock that Anne received as they drew up before the house and got out.

Emerging a couple of hours later through the old front door, they stood looking up at the dust covered windows – the same windows that Anne had gazed on with awe all those years before as a small child.

'We could manage – I suppose,' Anne pondered. 'It's a big thing. Rather frightening really, but I agree with you, we can't let it rot. We love it too dearly. Even if it isn't ours, it's the family home. And who knows who the real owner is. We don't and the trustees certainly don't seem able to make any headway. But I'm game, if you are, and I'm sure Mary and dear Gran will be too. How about it, brother Giles? What say you to the RAVENSWORTH TOWERS COUNTRY HOTEL? It sounds rather good, don't you think? Right then, shake on it. We're in partnership!' Anne's serious face took on one of its rare gleams, and almost shone with pure happiness. Giles was delighted.

How long they sat in Giles' car in front of the house, was hard to say. They just talked and talked. Away across the park, the lake shone in the afternoon sunlight and the home covert in the distance stood out in its new foliage which was just beginning to break. The park was taking on its spring clothes in readiness for yet another summer; a summer the young Ravensworths hoped would see the family restored to its old home.

'Well, this is where we must part,' they were back at the station, 'but as soon as I come out at the end of the year, I will get started on a full course at Cirencester, I've already written about it! We're going to need all the farming and estate knowledge we can muster, by the look of things, if we're to pull the place round. The trustees should be ashamed of themselves to have it go like this. I was wondering what to do, now I know!'

'Right, if you do that, then I'll do one in hotel management – but wait, will the trustees let us do this?'

'Leave it to Gran! So long, old girl.'

Tired and weary from her long day, Anne was thankful to sink down in a cosy armchair. From its depths, she unfolded her doings of the last twelve hours or so, and their plans for their future. It was a long story and Emily let her grand-daughter tell it in her own way, smiling quietly to herself as she listened. Looking up, Anne's eyes alighted on her grandmother's face and remained there.

'Gran. Oh, please, Gran; will you help us? Please?'

'I wonder . . .' Emily returned her grand-daughter's gaze, then half closed her own eyes. 'I don't see why not – we could do it – Mary will have to finish school first, but it will take time to arrange everything and repair it. It will have to be first class. But I could supervise that; maybe I could get the Dower House back and live there while the work's in progress. Then I'd be on the spot. All right, darling, I'll tackle the trustees in the morning. Leave it to me, Anne. Now off to bed, you're tired.'

How like Granny!

True to her word, Emily caught the early train to London the following morning. Seventy-five or no, she could still get her own way, and by the time she had finished with the trustees, they were only too thankful to concede to her wishes and allow the Ravensworths to return to their home and go ahead with their plans. There was plenty of money in the estate, and it needed a master to save it. One day, the trustees were sure, the heir would turn up, but in the meantime it might as well earn its own keep and be of some use. For Emily and her grandchildren would only be managers, the hotel would remain the trust's. Delighted with her morning's work, Emily returned on the afternoon train and phoned Mary that evening. Three years before, she had celebrated her ten years at the school with a whole holiday, and was now working for her general certificate. Hearing of their proposed return to Ravensworth, Mary was almost speechless with delight and excitement.

'Oh, Gran, do you really mean it? Are we really going back?' Mary, like all the others, had dreamt of the day when they would at last go home – for home meant Ravensworth. Now, with the new reign four years old and a Queen on the throne of England once again, the dream was coming true.

The next two years they were working for an end – it was both hard work and tremendous fun. Slowly the Towers recovered. Restored bit by bit to its former self, it once more had charm and dignity. The estate, too, slowly recovered from its years of mismanagement. It was uphill work, but by degrees they won. Emily's wish to return to the Dower House had also been fulfilled, for its short lease had fallen vacant that Michaelmas, allowing them home in time for Christmas. If they had rejoiced that Christmas, it was nothing to the rejoicing two years later, when they returned to the Towers itself.

Their return was naturally a just cause for a family reunion, and early in the New Year, Emily threw a welcome home party for all her many relations. It was like old times. At the end of the week, Emily was sad to see them depart, for Sarah returned with Harriet, with whom she was now going to make her home. With the departure of the last relation, the young Ravensworths rolled up their sleeves and got down to work.

Swiftly the weeks flew by, till only the sign remained to be fixed in its allotted place. The great morning dawned and amid much laughter and amusement, Giles fixed it up with due and fitting ceremony. It was Easter; they were in business!

Luck and good fortune had certainly been their guardian angels. For on their return to the estate they had found many willing people from the old days, only too thankful to return to the Towers and the family they had served for so many generations. Before long a loyal staff had gathered round them once again.

Nearly nine months had drifted by since that day, and the hotel had proved an undreamt of success. At long last the family were home and they were happy, content in the work they had chosen. What the future would hold for them, only time could tell, but in the meantime they asked for no better life than the one they were leading.

Emily opened her dark eyes, sat up very straight and looked at her sister-in-law on the far side of the fire. The embers were dying low, and outside the day was drawing in.

'Well, Maud. There you are. That's all.' She hesitated, and as an afterthought added with a wry smile. 'Lady Ravensworth!'

Maud's sunken green eyes danced with amusement and she, too, paused before replying.

'Why, if that isn't nice; now I suppose Giles will make me a dowager!'